Robert Jackson is a professor and a writer. He is a graduate of
Oxford University and has authored 46 books and hundreds
of newspaper articles. He was senior policy advisor to four
Canadian Cabinet Ministers.

Doreen Jackson is a writer and ski afficionado. They have
travelled widely to modern violence-prone areas and
peacekeeping missions, focusing on security and terrorism.
They currently live in California.

To our mothers,

Dorothy and Velma

Robert Jackson and Doreen Jackson

S K I

Corruption and Terror in Courchevel

AUSTIN MACAULEY PUBLISHERS™

LONDON • CAMBRIDGE • NEW YORK • SHARJAH

A CIP catalogue record for this title is available from the British Library.

ISBN 9781398440050 (Paperback)
ISBN 9781398440067 (ePub e-book)

www.austinmacauley.com

First Published 2022
Austin Macauley Publishers Ltd®
1 Canada Square
Canary Wharf
London
E14 5AA

Skiers know the joy and exhilaration of downhill descents. When that pleasure intersects with modern social and political change, there are unanticipated consequences. We watched in Courchevel 1850 as this was happening, and it was there that the germ of this story was planted. None of the characters are real, nor are the crimes. The hotel descriptions are fictional and not to be taken literally, as is the story itself. It is a magnificent resort area, a true jewel of France.

We are very grateful to the people who welcomed us to Courchevel so many times over the years, and to the many anonymous leaders who shared their views of how globalisation is impacting and changing French politics and culture.

Vive la France! Vive le ski!

Table of Contents

Between the idea
And the reality
Between the motion
And the act
Falls the Shadow

T S Eliot, *The Hollow Men*

"He had delusions and sundry humiliations. He saw a noble horse where others saw a decrepit animal.
He put a wash basin on his head and set out to battle like a knight."

Miguel de Cervantes, *Don Quixote*

This day and age we're living in
Gives cause for apprehension
With speed and new invention
And things like fourth dimension"

Herman Hupfeld, *Casablanca: As Time Goes By*

"Truth: Each man is entitled to as much of it as he can bear."

Nietzsche

Chapter 1
Violent Snowstorm

More than two feet of snow fell on Courchevel 1850 in the Alps that weekend. It was what the French call a *Tempête de Neige*, proof that nature has its own rules. Day and night the snow whirled and dropped silently, blanketing the woods and the craggy rocky slopes above the treeline with breath-taking beauty. The mysterious white stuff fell abundantly, erasing evidence of dirty grass, grey rocks, food cartons, beer bottles, dog manure, and even human blood. It gave no sign that something unknown, terrible, and unpredictable was about to happen.

Snowflakes are beautiful. Mankind has always been awed and mystified by their secrets. The Canadian Inuit have more than two dozen words to describe them, and although the Japanese have no word for intimacy, they have several for snow. The beauty of snow hides the fact that each crystal flake creates its own hexagon. Each has six corners with a unique singularity. The form of a snowflake is determined by the temperature, direction and strength of the wind, the altitude of the cloud, and other forces of nature. Once the six-pronged snowflake crystallises, it takes only minutes to fall through the sky, lose its original shape and vanish.

Snowflakes have much in common with people. They exist in our minds between memory and imagination. The trajectory of a single one parallels the spiritual course of a person. Each has its own individuality with an internal mysterious uniqueness. Snowflakes can be as soft and light as feathers, but when they fall too fast and thick, they coalesce, harden, distort images, and may even cause deadly harm.

Humans, too, are endowed with such inner and outer characteristics. Their original purity is transformed by degrees of unkindness, cruelty, and sometimes collective evil. Despite efforts to escape or hide, their lives are also extinguished by time, circumstance, and death.

Sometimes during that weekend in Courchevel 1850, the sky resembled the thick impenetrable fog or smog of the cold London dockyards, making it impossible to see beyond the base of the mountains. At other times, a 100-yard clearing was visible around the Croisette, the village centre of the exclusive Alpine ski resort. At night, only the glow of the blue neon hotel lights at the Chabichou, the faint green haze of the Pomme de Pin, and the muted red of the other village hotels reflected against sheets of virgin snow as it drifted down from the sky.

Despite nature's forbidding warnings to keep off the highest mountains in the Alps, French workers toiled to keep the picture perfect ski resorts open. It was the beginning of the Christmas season and every Savoyard knew that his or her livelihood and those of all the families in the area demanded that winter be beaten. But it was a difficult battle this year. Vehicles were stuck on mountain switchbacks and hairpin turns were blocked by drifting snow, fallen trees, and dislodged rocks.

For forty-eight hours, day and night, the winding roads leading up to Courchevel had been kept open by huge yellow and black cats and ploughs, closely followed by buses of anxious skiers and dozens of small trucks loaded with provisions of every kind. With tires carefully chained and windshields caked with ice and snow, the small *camions* carried urgent materials for the stores, restaurants, and hotels of the mountain resorts. Wine cellars were already stocked, but these trucks were loaded down with Perrier, Badoit, and Evian water bottles. The smaller vans brought fresh fish from Geneva, beef, pork and fowl from Grenoble; fresh produce and fine cheese from all the regions of France, but particularly from the area itself.

The chain of supplies wound its way up to Courchevel 1850. Named for its height in metres, this is the most lush, exclusive and expensive village in the Savoie region of France. For many, it is the finest ski resort in the world. The luxurious, glittering village is a major destination for world-famous skiers, movie stars and supermodels, a jewel that attracts Arab sheikhs, wealthy tycoons, international politicians, powerful mobsters, and spies and hitmen of every kind. It is an idealised sanctuary for some types of people. Some have jokingly called skiing in Courchevel 1850 a kind of fatal disease, especially those addicted to the thrill of extreme skiing and paragliding.

This enclave of privilege at the top of the mountain has on its doorstep the largest connected ski terrain in the world, the Three Valleys with miles of groomed runs and over 250 lifts. The ski area is equal in size to about the five top US ski resorts combined, offering 375 miles of downhill skiing. Within this huge domain, skiers can travel village to village, covering vast distances and seeking new destinations rather than simply going up and down the same mountain slopes. They can hurtle down black-diamond runs or ski leisurely on cross-country trails while they view panoramic snow-capped mountains and gaze on refracted light from the glaciers.

To house its wealthy guests, Courchevel 1850 possesses nine five-star hotels, and seven Michelin starred restaurants as well as several high-altitude restaurants scattered throughout the area. The best of the elite French ski school, the *Ecole de Ski Français,* or *ESF*, practises its trade here for the benefit of Europeans and hordes of wealthy international tourists from the Middle East, Russia, Japan, Britain, and America who pour into the village each ski week by automobile, train, and private plane from around the world.

A Christmas holiday there has been a ritual for many families for years, although the local merchants despair that, like every place else in Europe, the number of American travellers has dramatically declined since the end of the Cold War and the rise of international, radical Islamic terrorism. Many wealthy clients now gravitate instead to the security of North American luxury resorts like Aspen, Jackson Hole, and Whistler British Columbia with their plenitude of snow and safe surroundings.

The character of Courchevel 1850 changed dramatically over the years. It was always exclusive, with primarily European bourgeois and upper bourgeois clientele, but in the 1980s after the fall of the Soviet Union, that began to change dramatically. First Russians, then other super wealthy elites especially from the Middle East flowed in, sometimes literally bringing suitcases of cash. Joined by hedge fund managers and oil trading tycoons, many of the newcomers stayed in giant chalets, costing over $100000 a week complete with a private chef, butler and concierge. Unfortunately, they also brought with them many of the worst evils of large, cosmopolitan cities; debauchery, alcohol, drug abuse and crime. The ski village became a microcosm of the modern world elite, it was now top-heavy with the superrich and had relatively few lower middle and working-class clients.

The western European upper bourgeois still came, but they were often outnumbered. They guarded their high cultural activities like orchestral and theatrical productions in the Courchevel Forum, but raunchy nightclubs, open drug-use and nude pool parties competed, openly attracting many of the new rich and their followers. Old school Europeans were scandalised by the ostentatious and crude behaviour of the newcomers. Their own lives usually free of such baseness, contrasted vividly with the rebarbative renown of the new foreigners who had few financial limitations or moral prohibitions. What the old and new groups had in common was that they all came to escape something or someone.

Few ordinary would-be skiers are blessed with large enough bank accounts to stay at this highest and best equipped village on the mountain with its ultra-luxurious hotels and private chalets. Further down the mountain, there is a hierarchy of villages based on social class and measured by their height in metres above sea level. The farther down one goes, the cheaper the cost of lodgings. There is something for everyone somewhere.

Skiers of modest means, who are neither 'old-moneyed rich' nor 'new-rich', descend to Courchevel 1650 (Moriond) where they stay in less luxurious hotels or sometimes high-rise buildings. Skiers whose wallets are even thinner need to drop down to 1550 metres and stay at Courchevel Village with other lower middle-class families, primarily in large apartment complexes. Those who want to pay even less, and don't mind being far from the most prestigious ski runs and social action, go down even further to 1300 metres where they find humbler abodes in the village of Le Praz. Saint-Bon-Tarentaise, near the bottom of the mountain, and Brides-les-Bains, in the valley, also offer relatively inexpensive lodgings in bed-and-breakfast type accommodations.

These lower hamlets attract primarily younger skiers and working-class families who stay among the local French mountain workers and experience an enjoyable but different atmosphere. They often lack adequate dry snow, but there is always a bus up to a higher village where they can partake of the benefits of the upper villages, pristine slopes, uncrowded beginner runs, heart-in-the-throat black-diamond ski runs, ski-in ski-out shopping, late-night skidoo rambles, private helicopter rides, and thrilling hand-gliding and paragliding as well as gourmet restaurants and lively bars.

This weekend, as skiers struggled to arrive at the various Courchevel resorts, the chain of tractors, vans and cars ascended slowly up the hazardous mountain route, cutting crazy zigzag lines through the gusts of swirling snow. From above, it resembled a golden serpent crawling up toward a white heaven, bringing sustenance to a voracious, weather god. The vehicles drummed along, but their terrestrial ascent had no impact on the storm.

The blinding snow covered all but the highest jagged peaks of Courchevel 1850. The lower resorts of Courchevel as well as the outlying villages of Méribel, Les Menuires, and Val Thorens in nearby valleys were equally feeling the wrath of the god of winter. These family resorts were not blessed with as many wealthy foreign tourists nor as much a glitzy nightlife so they experience even blacker nights.

As the trucks full of provisions laboured to reach the ski station, their notoriously thin rubber wipers could not keep their windscreens cleared. Road signs proved impossible to read and the rattle of snow chains and straining engines obliterated even casual conversation. In the village of Courchevel 1850 itself, the deserted streets reminded the most seasoned villagers of the glorious winters of times past when blankets of snow covered the village and there were no automobiles, electricity, or even ski-lifts in the mountains.

Only occasional dynamite explosions punctuated the silence, unleashing manmade avalanches to dislodge unsafe mounds of snow in high elevations. The smell of wood smoke from traditional chalet fireplaces filled the air, but the storm deterred all animate life from venturing outside. Rabbits, squirrels and foxes hid deep in their holes, confined to live below the snow for most of the winter. At night only the giant black birds known as *choucas* flew and then only weakly, but purposefully, until they found a building where heat radiated from the chimney and onto the side of a wall. Their favourite place in Courchevel 1850 was the massive stone chimney at the Pomme de Pin hotel from where they could overlook the rich patrons pouring into and out of the festively lit Chabichou hotel and monitor the celebrations and shady goings-on in this wealthy part of town.

The large blackbirds rarely stirred from their warm resting place, and thus it was not surprising that they remained motionless when a door slammed behind a tall, warmly dressed man as he exited the Cat's Bar of the hotel Chabichou,

18

followed quietly by two very suspicious and dangerous looking characters. The auspicious duo was dressed as sombrely as the *choucas* themselves in dark winter parkas, with their black toques pulled down over their ears and eyes, hiding their faces. Their hands were thrust deep in their gun pockets.

The single man was Peter Worthington, recently arrived from England for his traditional ski holiday with his wife. Peter's head was down and he was deep in thought as he crossed the village to the foot of the Bellecôte ski run that wound up to his lodgings, the everyman's hotel, Courcheneige. The contrast between Peter and the two malevolent-looking men who followed him was dramatic, even farcical. A pleasantly pudgy, out-of-shape Brit, Peter was dressed as usual in chic English florescent – this year's style required large checks of every colour splashed in any direction as long as it made no rational sense. Since Brexit, the British middle-class knew that the country was in economic decline, but their optimism was boundless. This was most visible in young Londoners who continued to prefer the lively multicultural life of the city and its clubs to the colonial stuffiness of Whitehall and the Mall. All of them who could afford it flooded into France or further south for their winter holidays.

Locals noted that foreign visitors fit the same crazy, predictable pattern when they arrive at the village. Young or old, they act out fantasies of youth, wearing new wild, brightly coloured clothing. Many female adolescents with red pouty lips, florescent outfits, ultra-tight jeans and bunny boots do not even bother to ski. They love to frequent popular *après-ski* bars, where they drink the latest cocktails and dance to live music. The most famous place to hang out at Courchevel 1850 is the Bergerie, a bistro/bar on the Bellecôte ski run. During the day, young mothers hang out with their children on the sunny terrace, but at night, the venue transforms into a local meat-market for young and old alike.

As usual that night, Peter proudly sported a new *Les Trois Vallées* pass, allowing him to ski anywhere in the area. He adored the ski resort of Courchevel. For him, it was paradise on earth and his fondest memories were of his ski marathons in the interconnected valleys. He was not a great athlete, but like most foreign skiers who came to the resort, he prided himself on buying the most expensive pass which would enable him to use any of the 250 lifts and enjoy the thirty-mile run all the way from Courchevel via Méribel to Val Thorens and back again.

Of course, Peter rarely managed the marathon trip more than once during his two-week Christmas holiday. But when he did, it was a great triumph. It was not just his lack of stamina and skill that thwarted this accomplishment. Sue, his adorable and adored wife of forty years, also slowed him down. Peter never blamed or castigated her, but she had never mastered more than a slow, rudimentary, and not at all elegant stem christie. Since Peter rarely went anywhere without her, she managed to sabotage his heroic efforts to conquer the valley almost every time.

That night, Peter Worthington trudged slowly through the deep snow from the Chabichou hotel until he reached the lush Lana hotel at the base of the Bellecôte. It was cold and his mind was so fogged by alcohol and clogged with dark thoughts about what he had overheard in the Cat's bar that he mistakenly entered the Lana by way of the servants' door and had to work his way through a clutter of skis, boxes and clothing. Embarrassed, he literally stumbled into the grand foyer of the lavish hotel.

The Lana is a four-star hotel of 'grandstanding' on the west side of the Croisette in the centre of Courchevel 1850. Like many over-priced, expensive hotels in France, it possesses a bar that is resplendent with tarnished and fake *objets d'art* – a golden hawk, a golden palm tree laden with coconuts and other bizarre golden objects that are extremely grotesque but somehow seem to fit in hotels favoured by French stars of radio, television and films – in other words, by all those with little proven interest in serious reading or culture.

Peter brushed by the sexy starlets clustered at one end of the bar, oblivious of their presence. They barely glanced at him. The Lana's Brazilian bartender recognised Peter immediately as a regular and broke into a broad smile. Peter saluted him warmly, then moved to his usual opener. "How did your guests find the runs today?" He knew that the barman himself did not ski.

"Salut, Mr Worthington! Welcome back! It has been really bad out there. The snow was already deep from the storms of the past few weeks but it got much worse today with such terrible visibility. You couldn't see anything. The season is off to a terrible start. There have been all kinds of accidents – and I mean really awful accidents," the worker declared soberly as he doted on Peter as he did for every rich and out-of-shape tourist who came to the hotel. "I've never seen it so bad. So many people have died that I am beginning to wonder if those deaths were all accidents. Who knows? I probably shouldn't say so, but I'm suspicious."

Peter did not like the bartender's response after what he had just overheard in the Cat's bar. It made him queasy, suggesting a dark, even alarming picture of the ski resort – certainly an ill foreboding for his ski holiday.

Peter did not linger, and without ordering a drink nipped down to the back of the bar, pushed open the wooden gates and entered the toilet area. He was startled to find it already occupied by one of the men who had unsettled him so much earlier that evening at the Chabichou bar, discussing a sinister real estate deal and a lot of illicit skulduggery. The person sharing the loo was Baron de Rothschild, but Peter did not recognise him at first. All he saw was a tall white man with a purple penis and one huge testicle, groaning as he bent over a large, steel urinal. Peter had read about Adolph Hitler's distended testicle but he had never actually seen one before.

Taken aback by the bizarre sight, Peter's urge to relieve himself vanished, and he turned to heel and fled back to the bar where he immediately ordered a mind-numbing Capariso. He gulped it all down except the lime as he pondered whether the guy was ill or had simply burnt himself out on the slopes – or perhaps in bed.

Peter had never seen anything quite like it. Well, not quite. He recalled that last year in the luxury swimming pool at the Annapurna hotel, he had seen the same tall, slim Frenchman dunking himself violently in the whirlpool, and later moaning and repeatedly snapping his towel and hitting the wall with his fist in the steam room. It had startled Peter because he had never seen anyone express emotion so violently in a public place – at least not since his adolescence in an east London secondary school. But de Rothschild was totally different from Peter's former schoolmates. He normally looked

22

aristocratic, elegant and decidedly French, the way he had looked when he had stopped to chat up the two young girls earlier in the Cat's bar.

The man is bonkers, Peter thought. It flashed through his foggy mind that one never knows what lies beneath the multiple emotions that surface at a ski resort. All of life's contentment and misery can be found here. The cyclical seasons match the patterns of emotions in the Three Valleys; storms replace sunshine, happiness gives away to pain and violence. The mountain pleasures of hiking and biking during the dry summer days shift to new thrills and dangers on the snowy slopes in the winter. Snowflakes and skiers appear and then disappear as if they are of no importance or consequence.

The black mestizo bartender broke into Peter's reverie, asking if he wanted another round. Peter uttered his standard cliché: "*Merci, non.* Everyone can drink one Capariso but two is too many for anyone." Then he ventured an off-colour joke which he knew would be appreciated by a virile young man from South America. "What is the similarity between martinis and breasts?" Answering without waiting for a reply, Peter grinned. "One is not enough and three is too many." Proud of his wit, Peter paid the bartender a handsome tip, quickly left the Lana and began the next leg of the long trek up the Bellecôte ski run toward his hotel.

Chapter 2
Drunken Reveries and
Sober Realities

After his difficult hike up the mountain wading through the deep, ungroomed snow, Peter Worthington, the patriarch of British skiers in the popular Courcheneige hotel, was exhausted. He collapsed before the open fireplace and immediately ordered not one but two Armagnacs. After draining both snifters, Peter closed his eyes and allowed happy visions of his earlier years skiing in Courchevel to flicker through his mind before forcing his thoughts back to the conversation he had overheard at the Cat's bar.

His reveries transported him around the prestigious station, the largest ski area in the world, and the daunting and varied mountain terrain that surrounded it. In his many perilous trips up and down the most difficult runs in Menuieres, Val Thorens, and the Courchevels, he had seen it all. He smiled as he recalled his first breath-taking view of the area from the small airplane that had ferried him and his family from Geneva to their first ski vacation many years ago. He could still feel the exhilaration he had experienced as it landed at the tiny picturesque *altiport* perched on the side of the mountain. He envisaged his first trips up the Sommet de la Saulire and the splendid outings with his boys to and from Saint-Martin-de-Belleville on the icy Jerusalem run. There was no doubt these ski vacations had been the best times his whole family had experienced together.

During his long Three Valley runs, he had often thought about the area as it must have been decades before the arrival of modern skiing. Outside the major resorts that cover only an exiguous part of the local terrain, today's languid atmosphere revealed majestic and pastoral beauty, but also sadness for what was once here. A musty smell of decay permeated the few desolated remains of previous lives; poverty, deserted homes, run-down shepherds' huts, and dilapidated stone mission churches. Staring into this strangeness, Peter could understand the defiance, gloom, and even despair that the inhabitants of earlier years must have found in the landscape. He could also feel how the evasion and escape that used to be possible in this peaceful countryside had been replaced by modern stress, injury, corruption and even death.

As Peter glanced around the room now, he could imagine the first Frenchman he had met at the hotel Courcheneige, the rude one who demanded that the waiter apologise for serving a cold fish for dinner. The trout was tepid, and after the man's sharp rebuke to the headwaiter, the chef was forced to re-cook it. "We have been coming here for 15 years, and when you bring friends, you expect proper service or you don't pay!" the Parisian had complained loudly.

Peter and his family always were scandalised by such rude behaviour. It was often ugly Americans who bothered them, but no one disturbed him more than the unbearable, and pushy French – though he did marvel at how they always got their way. Peter concluded that the French must always be rude on vacation. It seemed to him that they were always the ones with the best seats on the terrace, in the dining room, and around the swimming pool. His exquisite humility hampered his understanding of the French bourgeoisie and others who always looked after themselves first. "We know less than we think we do" was his only response.

In school, Peter, had been nicknamed Falstaff because he loved observing people and found pleasure in finding chinks in their personalities and then exploiting them. He enjoyed the comic side of life – unplanned, chaotic, and messy. He rarely wore a ski hat or toque. Whenever he was asked why he was not properly dressed for the cold weather, he would respond with a smile and the same determined phrase "to give my head a chance". He believed that life is not rich enough in its rare comedy, so laughs should be cherished and hoarded for bad days. As an aging man he got up each day astonished to see himself and pleased that he had survived another night.

Being unreservedly generous by nature, Peter was always ready to praise others. He was characterised by an unfashionable normality. He did not have strong opinions or angry convictions and tended to understand and sympathise with everyone. Unlike many people today, he did not think that those who differed from him were ill-informed, unintelligent or acting in bad faith. Instead, he lusted after life and believed that enjoyment or happiness was all there was. "The afterlife can look after itself," he would declare after a few drinks and made everyone around him want to adopt the same *carpe diem* attitude. But he was also an astute judge of people and found some of them envious and ignoble.

Peter was mild mannered and compassionate. The kind of man who would not hurt a fly. He held fast to unfashionable principles of high morality, the Church of England, truth-telling, British patriotism, the monarchy, and the constitution. His search for truth and sensitive curiosity always led him to choose self-sacrifice over selfishness.

For good or bad, this complete honesty was a product of vast experience with others at work and play. Like many Englishmen, if Peter saw people being hurt, he felt obligated to rush to their rescue. He regarded 'proper' behaviour as the mark of a civilised person. Perhaps this was why he was so upset over what he had overheard at the Chabichou hotel. He knew it was none of his business but it bothered him deeply, nonetheless.

Peter sighed deeply. On arrival at his hotel earlier that evening, he had been very despondent because of the bad weather and while Sue rested, he had gone to the famous hotel to console himself with a few drinks at his favourite bar. The Cat's Bar was a kind of play on words with the name of the hotel – Chabichou – but Peter liked to explain that although it sounded like a 'chat' (or cat), the word actually referred to a cheese made in the Burgundy region of France. That night Peter had chosen the Cat's because he longed for the familiar, relaxing swing music of the Vitamine Jazz band that always played at the hotel over the Christmas season.

Peter forced his thoughts back to what he had seen and heard in the bar just before he headed back to the Lana hotel and then up the mountain to his own more modest hotel.

He played and replayed in his mind the scene as he had entered the bar. After saying hello to Dick Major, the piano player – an ex-American from California who lived with his

Swedish wife in the Dordogne area of France – Peter took his customary seat in the far corner of the main bar to enjoy his favourite American jazz. In rusty French, he ordered a Campari-Orange and sat back to relax and enjoy the fun of the evening along with the enchanting sound of the band leader's red clarinet.

Peter could remember feeling fed up. He had arrived by airplane that afternoon with high hopes that were rapidly fading. The weather these years was terrible. Last Christmas he had tried four times to ski from Courchevel to Val Thorens, but had not made it even once. While he sometimes blamed the weather or more likely Sue, he had to admit to himself that it was not all their fault. The truth was that at age of 75, he was becoming scared to death of plunging down the difficult twists and turns on the steep runs that were required for a complete Three Valley run. He had a sad but clear idea about his own physical decline. Both his parents had died before their 70th birthday.

On reflection, Peter knew that he had to face up to the seriousness of what he had heard at the Chabichou bar, but it was difficult for him. When he had arrived there that night, it had been quite full despite the storm and late hour. There were several Arabs in the far corner of the room, including a young family at one table and two very well-dressed men, probably from Kuwait or Saudi Arabia, or perhaps from Iraq or Syria, at another. He remembered that the veiled woman and young boy drank orange juice and the bearded man with her ordered a Coca-Cola with the best whiskey. Clearly his prohibitions were different here than at home. Two more men in the middle of the room, who looked Italian or perhaps Russian, were drinking whisky straight-up.

Peter also remembered two slim young women huddled somewhat awkwardly on a sofa close to him. Not far from them, a young, well-turned-out chick with a stylish mink jacket cut a different figure. She was obviously drawn there with hopes of enticing the kind of rich, single men who frequented the bar.

The music quickly cast its spell, and after a second Campari, Peter began to swoon to the music. François Rocard, the French clarinettist, was terrific. He played many instruments, but the melodious red clarinet brought out the best in him. After a few introductory bars on the piano by Dick, François would blow out a sweet sound and swing to the jazz beat. At the end of every piece he laughed out a *voila du travail* with which the audience gradually began to chime in, as a sign of familiarity in the Cat's bar.

The room was furnished with light brown, comfortable leather chairs. Peter had always thought them overly rich and elegant for a ski lodge. To him they sat curiously under the strange images on the wall behind him; the four familiar, softly lit murals with five almost human figures in different shades of red. Two of the images were of jazz band players but the remainder were beyond easy description. If Peter had tried to describe them, he would have said they reminded him of a man sticking a cigarette in someone's ear. But no one ever did.

As he ordered a third Campari-Orange from the Cat's barman, Peter became aware of the elegant accents of three men speaking French in a dark corner booth behind him. Probably because Peter looked and sounded English, they paid no attention to him. They obviously assumed he spoke no French and made undisguised, rude remarks about his accent and all the drunken, lower-class Brits who had "taken over" the ski runs and bars.

These rude remarks soured Peter's mood and he listened much more carefully to their conversation than he normally would have. One of them was definitely not French, Peter thought. His appearance and manner gave him away. He was Asian, perhaps Japanese. Although he was dressed immaculately in a perfectly tailored suit and spoke brilliant French, he looked stiff and out of place in the bar. Whoever he was, he joined in none of the rude comments about the English but just listened intently to his companions' jokes and complaints.

From their conversation, Peter discovered that the short Asian was Inoyne Watanabe who represented TIM – the leading Tokyo Investment Management Corporation known for its shady dealings in global money transactions. Peter knew from his own business connections that the firm specialised in using capital from Japan and other countries to buy properties around the world, particularly in America and Europe. Registered in New York and Dusseldorf, its activities were famous, if not notorious, for high yielding investments and unsavoury financial deals. The firm possessed outstanding financial backing in Tokyo and Osaka. It was closely connected with the governing Liberal Democratic party of Japan and its sister parties around the world.

The second man was French and seemed wealthier, but, for some reason, was also obsequious to the third man in the white turtleneck. The taller person, Peter realised from his many previous visits to the area, might be Charles de Rothschild, a Courchevel regular and one of the leading businessmen in France. Peter had often seen him around the resort. He, too, was known for big international business deals. His clothes were of a very fine cut, purchased perhaps in the fashionable Louis Vuitton store on Boulevard Saint Germain in Paris. He appeared overly intent on pleasing the second shortest member of the group.

Peter smiled despite himself as his mind skipped back to the bizarre scene later in the evening in the men's toilet at the Lana hotel. He concluded that the man in both instances was indeed de Rothschild, a demented, bisexual French man. Who would have guessed that he was both a wealthy businessman and a psychological nutcase?

The third man was definitely French. He was short and also smart-looking, except for the shape of his nose which Peter thought resembled the curved angle of the ski jump in the centre of Courchevel 1850. He wore a dark suit and a white turtleneck sweater. Peter recognised him as a widely known politician and Cabinet minister, *Monsieur le Ministre* Lionel Jospin. He was clearly running the conversation.

Jospin, Peter knew, was in charge of the three major police forces in France as well as the Direction Centrale du Renseignement Interior, known colloquially as RG which was tasked with counterespionage, counterterrorism and domestic intelligence. It was one of the most capable and feared security forces in the world with close connections to legal organisations such as Interpol and the CIA as well as illegal ones such as the European mafia.

Jospin was very familiar with this region because he was the former Member of Parliament from the Haute Savoie, the geographical and political region of Courchevel. In the conversation, he was explaining to the Japanese investor, Watanabe, about the intricacies of skiing in the French Alps, lecturing him on the finer points of French haute cuisine at Courchevel 1850, and also how to enjoy the high life in Paris. Watanabe, however, looked a trifle irritated and kept bringing the conversation back to the details of the financial deal he wanted to discuss.

Like many outstanding Japanese investors, Watanabe spoke excellent French. Peter knew he had graduated from both Sciences Politiques and the National School of Administration in Paris and knew France inside out. He told Jospin that he was impatient to conclude their deal so that he could get back to Tokyo where he was needed. His wife, it appeared, was nursing his daughter through very tough examinations to enter the Kyoto Law School.

The conversation suddenly turned to ski properties in the Savoie. Watanabe had been supremely successful in real estate deals in the west of Canada. In fact, he had made a fortune for his company. He was practically responsible for a popular Canadian saying that there are only two things to see in Banff, elks and Japanese. The truth was somewhat more complicated, but it was clear that Watanabe, with some help from the New York branch of TIM Corporation in New York, had drawn on billions of dollars' worth of surplus Japanese yen in the United States to buy most of the famous ski resort. It had made international headlines when the mighty Canadian Pacific Corporation finally sold the Banff Springs hotel, succumbing like other lesser establishments to the highest bidder. The Alberta resort today, Peter reflected, was primarily Japanese, covered with bilingual signs, Japanese and English, and boasted four pricey Japanese restaurants.

"The yen is so vital to Canada's weak economy that the new minority Conservative government is even considering selling off the national park itself," Peter recalled Watanabe proudly announcing to his audience.

However, Jospin, like many French politicians, ignorantly considered himself an expert on Canada and he stopped Watanabe's discourse in full flight. "France is not like Canada, you know," he had said smugly. "Buying property here is more complex. We have no free trade agreement with the United States and you can't just use your surplus capital in this country as you please. Things have to be arranged..." He trailed the later point off in a condescending manner, implying, but not actually stating, Peter thought, that he and his government friends would have to get their proper financial share of any deal concerning buying property in France, and particularly in his fiefdom, the Savoie, or the notorious security service would be used to ensure they would.

De Rothschild had intervened at that point to prevent Watanabe from 'losing face' by this overtly blunt remark. Reaching into his immense briefcase, he had pulled out a slick publicity brochure advertising the French Alps. The glossy pictures showed beautiful young, and not so young, athletes and celebrities on ski runs around the village. Some were skiing lazily down easy, well-groomed slopes, while others were captured hurtling down difficult runs and executing sharp, dangerous curves over huge moguls that ranged as far as the eye could see. The excitement, even drama, of skiing at such a place shone through the pages.

"These gems," he said pointing to hotel photos in the pamphlet, "are what we are after." Splendid coloured pictures of the most expensive hotels and glittering shops in the area seem to lift right off the glossy paper.

The discussion had then turned to the hotels themselves, and Peter gathered that despite, or perhaps because of, their huge investments and need for continual upgrades, there were several five-star hotels already up for sale. Some were modern, others rustic. In the pictures, all were nestled under beautiful trees laden with snow, and highlighted guests who were international celebrities and politicians who had flown into Courchevel from around the world. The two largest and most valuable hotels were the Annapurna and the Byblos de Neige.

Peter knew the Annapurna well, a beautiful hotel resort nestled on a slope just above the village. It had its own ski lift and direct access to the precarious-looking mountain *altiport* or airstrip he had first arrived on. It was the preferred hotel of the non-western elite. Frequented by sheikhs from the Gulf States, United Arab Emirates, Kuwait, Qatar, Oman, Saudi Arabia, and some Russians, it had run into hard days after the Iraqi invasion of Kuwait and the subsequent wars with western states in the Middle East in Iraq, Libya, Syria, and Yemen.

The three men had gone on to talk about how hot wars and frozen violent conflicts are not good for business, and even the Annapurna Parisian Chef had deserted the hotel for more money on the Mediterranean coast. Worse, the property was no longer impeccably maintained and the rooms no longer reflected the royal style to which patrons in the past had been accustomed. Even its beautiful wood-burning fireplaces were often left unattended and unlit. In spite of these handicaps, the asking price for this exclusive hotel and all its possessions, including the *altiport*, was almost a billion and a half euros, or one billion times .272257 Emirati Dirhams, Peter had calculated on his iPhone.

But there was another hotel under discussion among the men. Located in the middle of the *Jardin Alpin,* or Garden of the Alps, a wooded area in the centre of all the ski runs above the centre of the village, the Byblos de Neige possessed the choice location and arguably the best rooms of the whole village. The Byblos des Neige was only slightly less exclusive than the Annapurna, but the men indicated that in the current situation many real estate agents thought it should sell for more. Peter knew that hotel too. He and Sue had planned to stay there when the children no longer came with them. Every suite had its own fireplace tended with fresh firewood daily. Freshly cut flowers filled the vases, the champagne buckets were kept replenished with Lanson Black Label Brut, and the minibars were stocked with several varieties of vodka.

Despite its tired lobby and somewhat rundown exterior, very rich western Europeans continued to come there when they could scrape up more than $1000 per day per person for a room or an even more expensive suite, and when there was enough snow in the area to make the price worthwhile. With warmer winters that was never certain. Recently, it was the Russians, mobsters, spies, and hitmen who frequented the place. They liked the ski valets and pre-heated boots. The thought made Peter smile. He had heard rumours that the French security service had placed eavesdropping equipment in all the priciest rooms.

The feature that Peter liked best was that the Byblos boasted the second best and rowdiest piano bar in the region. The best was the Cat's, but other top bars could be found even in smaller three and two-star hotels.

Of course, there were other nights spots. The area was studded with elegant casinos along with other cheaper taverns and hangouts, including the notorious Bergerie famous for its Friday night celebrity meat market. Partying, soaking in hot stubs, and drinking were as important as skiing, so hotels with their own 'watering holes', such as the Byblos, were favoured, especially now that the police were hanging out on the slopes with breathalysers and giving drinking tickets.

Peter recalled how in the hotel bar Watanabe had tried to get back in Minister Jospin's good graces after the latter's putdown about real estate deals in France. The Japanese businessman had tried to explain the new position he found himself in. "Sir, I agree with everything you have said, but don't forget the Japanese yen is no longer very strong so we have to find other means of obtaining the necessary capital." He hesitated then glanced around the room as he said quietly: "We may even need to get funds from the Russians. If necessary, we can even use our mafia contacts."

Peter had had difficulty containing himself as the pretentious Minister growled back viciously and without warning, "Let's get it straight, slant eyes. The President gets a ten percent cut of this deal or it won't happen. Simple as that! It is a principle with him. It's up to you to get the capital. It is not our business to get it for you. If you need to deal with the Russian mafia, just do it."

Watanabe looked shaken. "Are you sure the owners will all sell? What if they won't?" he asked. "We need certainty."

"We've invested a lot in, shall we say…inducements…so we don't expect too much trouble." Jospin had smiled, but his face was cold in a firm ministerial manner. At that moment, he had glanced over at Peter and their eyes met. "Time to go," he growled, and stood up. As he left, he had said to Watanabe, "Just do your part before we meet again!" The group dispersed and left the bar except for de Rothschild who sidled over to where the two awkward girls were sitting and lingered there for a few moments before departing.

In his current drunken state back in the Courcheneige hotel, Peter now wondered if he really had heard this discussion. He was weary to his bones after working right up to his flight from London. Had he been too drunk to understand what they had been saying? Could it have been as sinister and violent a plot as he recalled?

Had such international crooks replaced the spies and thieves of the Cold War? If his memory and analysis was valid, Courchevel was about to experience a new normal – modern criminal corruption at its worst including big businessmen, high-ranking government officials, fearless security police, and even murderous mafia. This new generation of transnational thieves and crooks would also include the modern rich who move their money around the world from country to country, continent to continent and hide their wealth from public scrutiny by manipulating and laundering it.

Was his imagination running wild? Had the mafia, terrorists, politicians and their business associates, who had picked on soft targets such as entertainment institutions in London and Paris, now moved to targets such as skiing resorts? He was uncertain, but it felt like corruption in paradise to him.

Peter loved and knew this part of the Alps well. But it was changing. He roused himself from his reveries. *When it snows in the mountains it always hides things*, he thought. But what?

He knew that British MI6 agents often said that more can be learnt about criminals by studying their outward appearances than by just listening to their words, but he was deeply suspicious about what these men had said. All skiers look the same, he mused, but you never know what is going on in their minds. Just like you never know what is under the surface of the snow. Something very sinister might be lurking there. He had felt a twinge of dread after hearing the menacing undercurrent of their conversation, but was it warranted? Could they harm him or his wife, Sue? *Not everything that seems obvious is true*, he thought. *But not everything that is true is obvious either*, he concluded.

"*Garçon*, another cognac, please," he called to the Courcheneige bartender. He then pulled out his cell phone and attempted to call an American journalist and skiing friend Robert Arnett, who was staying in the nearby ski hamlet of Méribel. There was no answer so he left Arnett a brief message summarising what he had overheard. Then he suggested that the two of them should share a drink at the British pub tomorrow after their first ski class so that he could tell him more and get his advice about what, if anything, he should do about it.

Chapter 3
The Sordid Underside of
the Ski Resort

Much is hidden beneath the surface of an international ski resort, both under the snow and far below the happy social scene. Dangers like blue ice, jagged rocks, accidents, avalanches, petty crime and sometimes even murder are lurking just out of sight. Resort pleasure-seekers are all familiar with the routine theft of ski equipment and the filth under new snow, but modern ski complexes mask much worse abominations. Even the galleys of the grand hotels and the machines that transport skiers up and down the mountain hide secrets from holidaymakers.

There is an underworld, or an underlife if you will, to skiing. People are often repelled by the lack of cleanliness of mountain toilets but they can be spotless compared to the hidden parts of hotels. Under and around the seasonal kitchens, garbage deposal areas are often full of moisture, slime, bacteria and insects. Laundry rooms, too, are regularly filthy, piled with heaps of stained towels and bedding soiled with cigarette ashes, decayed urine and occasionally semen. After dark, the local rats come out to clean up the messes throughout the resorts and now that vermin in places like Paris have their own human lobbying and interest groups protecting them, it is difficult for local authorities to employ the most deadly poisons to kill them.

Ski travel brochures show glitzy hotels with fancy restaurants and bars, but too often the reality is shrunken rooms, watered-down drinks, and imported mass-produced food. When skiers wander out of their hotels in search of beauty and tranquillity, they find mainly shops with overpriced goods, staffed with underpaid assistants in search of a romantic fling with someone – anyone – to escape the boring existence of their lives. However, it all contributes to the modern illusion that only the surface of life matters.

Every large ski station also has an industrial heartland that is hidden from the alpine wonderland's busy lifts and runs by heavily treed hills or valleys. At Courchevel 1850, that complex is housed in a building that is officially called the Cachemire Edifice, named after the German who built it, but the French locals call it simply *le cauchemar* or nightmare. It is a spooky place that tells you that just because you are paying for an expensive resort you are not necessarily safe.

Outside the buildings, behind the trees and mountains of dumped snow, are all the electricity cables and telephone wires that connect the village to the energy grid and the world. Inside the corrugated huts, one finds the hidden equipment that keeps the lifts running, the snow tractors purring, and the skimobiles functioning. Slick and dirty materials are kept on-hand for the perpetual oiling, greasing, and repairing of ski equipment. The workers in these huts have seen everything – defective equipment, damaged lifts, thick grease spills, soiled underwear, tangled hair, blood, even skin and bones. They are hardened cynics who joke about the absolute safety of the lifts as guaranteed by the owners and Albert Jospin, the government minister for the region.

The beauty of ski resorts also often hides an underworld of corruption, criminality, and human treachery. While a ski holiday enhances opportunities to meet people from different social classes and countries, it also provides the anonymity of a large city. Revellers are free to act out their fantasies. Petty criminals work the slopes and luxury stores while prostitutes frequent the hotels and bars. This year at Courchevel 1850 was no exception, but the variety of criminals – political henchmen, international investors, French politicians, jihadi terrorists, and Russian mafia – was startling and new.

A ski resort often resembles a 'ship of fools', or what Shakespeare's *King Lear*, in his darkest hour, termed a 'stage of fools'. As the storm abated on this first day of Christmas ski week at Courchevel 1850, whispered conversations and rumours about unusual accidents and deaths abounded, although life on the surface continued as usual.

For many visitors, luxury resorts are about flaunting lots of money, especially on drinks, exotic food, shopping, and sex. This year, as usual, some very rich and would-be rich individuals had come to Courchevel 1850 expressly for an auction of expensive jewellery and paintings in the lower Croisette. For their pleasure, the *Diamant Centre* boutiques next-door were packed with luxury goods of every sort – caviar, *pate de foie gras*, shirts for the 'man who does the impossible', glittering party dresses, and paintings by the famous Claude Schirr (an especially costly one was *La Terrasse du Festival*, wonderful from a distance but migraine-inspiring from close-up).

Unusual characters often trail the resort's wealthy foreign clientele here, hovering particularly in front of the *Diamant* entrance. Today, for example, a middle-aged woman, with too much lipstick and dressed in an old fur coat, was seen trying to pawn off a worthless ten franc note as a collector's item. An elderly, frail veteran in full military regalia sat with cup on a bench by the creperie asking for money for food. Close by, in front of a Spanish restaurant, an elderly crippled woman in a red hat made her way slowly across the terrace, undeterred by the snowstorm or posted warnings about thieves in the area.

Bizarrely, this latter octogenarian, dubbed by locals as the Zucchini Woman, always came at the same hour, routinely ordered the same food, and ate it in the same precise order at the same table; coffee, three small glasses of tomato juice, then boiled zucchini. She had lived in the village for decades, but little was known about her except that she was eccentric and seemed to know everything and everybody. That fall, she had been spotted removing wilted but still blooming flowers from a trash bin in the cemetery, then placing them on the grave of a man who had died recently in mysterious circumstances.

The woman's physical handicap, sharp intellect, and regular presence in the heart of the village made her privileged to things that others did not know. A curious observer might have asked many questions. What was she doing out in such terrible snow conditions? Was it just the habit or custom of a keen observer of all that went on in the ski station or something else? Did she have any insights into the weird and deadly accidents that had plagued the region for months?

Every Savoyard, including the Zucchini Woman, was all too aware that this was a bizarre and dramatic opening to the winter season. After a series of early crippling storms, the latest blizzard had topped off the longest and worst December in the Savoie area since the end of the Second World War. The unusual weather had brought with it a series of disasters, some easy to explain, others not. The disconnected events confused experts and amateurs alike. It was every skier's nightmare.

In early December, there had been several deadly avalanches in the region. These events in themselves were not unusual, but their severity was surprising, so that some sceptics had even called for a police investigation and protection because of the high number of fatalities. Such deadly cascades of snow are neither as rare as one might think, nor are they simply acts of God. Steep terrain, snow conditions and human behaviour are all implicated in setting them off. Experts do their best to make the mountains safe by creating controlled avalanches, but many, like the deadly ones in the Haute-Savoie that week, are triggered by the victims themselves, often by young, inexperienced skiers who venture off the groomed runs showing off to their peers.

The avalanches in France so far this season had overwhelmed the emergency crews and dominated the local news for days. Predicting and controlling such events is not an exact science, so good skiers know they must be well informed. High altitude skiers are advised to wear special beacons that are able to send and receive radio signals allowing victims to be found quickly, even under deep heaps of snow. However, in none of the recent cases were the accident victims properly equipped. Some just didn't know better; others claimed their gear had been stolen.

Search and emergency rescue teams were forced to use traditional methods to locate survivors and bodies, working in tandem with trained rescue dogs. Sticks and bare hands were too often their final resort in the frantic race to locate people deep under the snow. They drove seven-foot-long probes into the snow in search of air pockets that might keep the victims alive. In a few cases, skiers lucky enough to have been buried in an air pocket have been found alive as long as three days after the accidents, but this year none were.

The mammoth avalanches near the neighbouring resorts of Val d'Isère and Tignes were the worst in French history. At the Val, an unexpected torrent of snow careened thousands of feet from cliffs above the town, smashed into buildings, and ripped through a chalet killing two young children whose parents were helping to dig out stranded automobiles in the quartier. At Tignes, the avalanche was self-inflicted. A group of naïve skiers had set it off while ignoring the rules and skiing *hors piste* in unstable snow. The broken bodies of the survivors were stabilised and transported by helicopter to the largest nearby hospital at Albertville to be treated for trauma and hypothermia.

Of course, a number of such accidents are expected over a ski season in any resort. It is a risky sport. The previous year there also had been many unplanned avalanches with several dozen serious accidents in the region, but only a small fraction of them had resulted in deaths. Usually, the victims came away with broken bones, sprains, and bruised and wounded egos. But this year, there were more fatalities and several strange and inexplicable accidents in the mountains.

44

In fact, in the weeks just ahead of Christmas there were so many more horror stories than usual that even the normally nonchalant French police were alarmed. They calculated that during the first two weeks after the ski lifts opened, there had been more than three times as many serious and unexplained incidents as in similar periods in previous years, and almost half of them differed from the usual types of accidents. It didn't take long for this concern to be picked up by local officials and even the media, then widely disseminated and exaggerated.

The ski incident that had created an uproar in the press and on the Internet in early December was a horrific, pre-season crash of the huge cable car at the top of the craggy *Sommet de la Saulire*, one of the highest mountains in France. This popular cable car could carry up to 250 persons, making it the largest single ski lift in the world. At the height of the ski season, masses of skiers pack together in lifts like this. A product of the best engineering design, the cable car had not experienced even a single day's delay in service since its inauguration twenty years earlier.

During a storm just three weeks before Christmas, as the *téléphérique* swung up the last leg of its journey, a sudden violent blast of wind had struck the giant train-like box with such force that it dislodged the lift from the steel cable. It crashed to the ground, then slid backwards, rolling over the rocks and jagged peaks onto a busy ski run. Inside there was carnage. People screamed as their bodies were brutally bashed about inside the enclosed lift. Horrified skiers below said the screams from the box car were even louder than the grating sound of the ski lift as it hurtled over rocks, dropped onto the

45

Vizelle piste and then finally lodged at the last pylon before a restaurant at the halfway place.

The next day, newspapers reported that the passengers – mostly workers in the ski industry and apartment owners with young children – had violently slammed into each other. Eyes had been jabbed by flying poles as the tumbling mass of flesh and bones smashed into each other. One report claimed that a loose ski nearly decapitated a 25-year-old British kitchen helper, who only the day before had bragged to his buddies about his masculine prowess in terrifying others on the ski slopes.

At first, the investigators thought that the computer control centre for the giant lift had been sabotaged, but the only available evidence indicated that a glitch in one of the master chips, combined with the stress of a sudden blast of wind, had caused an electric circuit to fault, leading directly to the disaster. A board of enquiry hastily concluded that this was a terrible accident, but nothing more. People were not to blame, it said: a faulty Russian-made chip and French equipment were the culprits.

After the accident, authorities made every effort to halt the media frenzy that was spreading well beyond Courchevel 1850. The station owners immediately bought another huge lift from the manufacturer in industrial Grenoble and replaced the faulty Russian computer chip with a similar device from Moscow. They also launched massive publicity efforts to contain the damage done to their reputation. Even French President François Marchand was enlisted to calm nerves. "Such events are unnatural at the Courchevel ski resort in the French Savoie," he declared pompously on television. "It was a terrible accident, caused by a freak storm. All is now well taken care of."

Despite the fact that 10 adults and 5 children had died and 140 more had been severely injured in the accident, the ski season was proceeding as if nothing had happened. However, a degree of suspicion lingered. Many people cancelled their reservations, but others arrived, with varying degrees of trepidation.

Despite the government's reassurance, some foreboding signs continued. Two days before the official season was to begin, one of the Courchevel 1850 egg lifts (or bubbles as the English called them) was ripped violently from its lift line in a wild roar of wind and tumbled down the ski run to the village of Le Praz at 1300 metres, some five hundred metres below Courchevel 1850. Fortunately, no one was in the lift at the time, nor were there many people on the slopes. The storm had kept almost everyone, even most locals, hunkered down in their chalets and hotels.

Perhaps the most ominous and perplexing death in the village of Courchevel 1850 came to light on the day before Christmas week opened. A giant snowplough, which was in the process of removing five feet of snow behind the cinema, accidentally pushed a badly parked, small, yellow car over the cliff down towards the lower Courchevel Village 1550. When the buried car was located, the authorities found a dead woman in it. Her body had been covered with bed sheets, but her throat had been slit and blood was splattered all over the inside of the car. As one creative reporter put it, more than the god of winter was sinister this year at Courchevel.

Every skier knows that accidents are part of the excitement and challenge of their sport. They also know that deaths by avalanches, lift accidents, and ski mishaps are relatively rare. Skiers also tend to be fearless because they believe that serious accidents and deaths always happen to someone else, not them. They are too skilled; too careful. They also know that broken bones and other minor accidents for the less skilled are easily mended in a busy and convenient *cabinet de médecine* in the heart of the village. In worst case scenarios, helicopters can be relied upon to rescue them if, by some remote chance, they get into trouble skiing off groomed runs. At worst, they think, if they ever did become a victim, they would have a lifetime of bragging rights about their harrowing adventure. So, no worries!

By the time the Christmas season formally opened that Saturday and tourists were trickling in, everything appeared to be getting back to normal. And it was, at least on the surface. The lifts were oiled, checked, re-checked, and running smoothly. Snow was abundant. The ski instructors were in form and anxious to work, and the hotels were fully staffed and at their best. While some hardy skiers were upset that yet another snowstorm had arrived to restrict them from skiing as far afield as they wanted, there was also an expectation that superb conditions would soon follow.

Until Monday, only the most adventurous athletes ventured very far outdoors. Visibility was poor, planned avalanches were being unleashed and slopes were constantly being groomed and regroomed. In the chalets that weekend, anxious children who had made it to the resorts were bored and complained to their family and friends about the lack of activity. Men bitched to their wives about how much it was costing to sit indoors, and energetic teenagers looked for any kind of trouble. But the vast majority read books, absorbed yesterdays' newspapers, played video games, cards, bridge, scrabble, and drank a lot of alcohol.

Old timers worked on their business accounts, agendas, diaries, and made new lists. One such geezer, intrigued by the unusual beginning to this season, made notes while peering out at the storm. He happily announced to his wife, "Now, I keep my diary but one day it will keep me. This year is one for the history books." The sentiment was not original. As usual, during the longest and most severe storms, the seasoned Brits at the Hotel Courcheneige preferred not to think about skiing; they were content just to drink. Younger clients found solace in exploring the sewers of the Internet.

Despite the weather, skiing always reaches crescendos during the short high seasons in late December and mid-March each year. People who love the mountains are united by a high degree of optimism. It is as if they accept, even celebrate, the present with its superficial daily needs and wants, and prefer to ignore the risks, rules of nature, life, injuries and death, or whatever is under the surface of their humdrum lives.

Chapter 4
Friends and Enemies in
the Ski School

Monday, December 22, offered the beginning of a new season with the formal opening of the Christmas ski week. The day rose cold and snowy, but by midmorning it had warmed so that the light, new powder at the bottom of the runs was already a mix of slush and corn snow. By then, of course, experienced skiers were long gone – off to face the challenge of skiing in fog on one run and sunshine on the next. For them, the best times on the mountains are always as close as possible to sunrise and sunset.

The most adventurous skiers are prepared to do whatever is necessary to get a head start. At sunrise when the runs are empty and often blanketed with new snow, it is the perfect time to sneak an early ride to the top. By ten am when lessons start, the lifts and runs become crowded. It stays like that until late afternoon, when average skiers are tired, even exhausted, and desert the mountain runs for the spas, bars and restaurants where they evolve from aggressive, tired skiers into party animals. Beginners, on the other hand, tend to keep their heads bowed and knees rigidly bent as they fight for just one more run before darkness and closed lifts force them to retire and rest their tired legs. The experts are the last down the mountain. They push on and on for just one more magical experience before the sun has hidden behind the tallest peaks and the snow sweepers make their last run to clear everyone off the slopes.

After years of frustrating, sporadic efforts to ski in deep powder without formal instruction, Peter Worthington had finally signed up for the expert class that morning. It was not an easy decision because it meant leaving his darling wife to fend for herself on the bunny slopes, in town or on the sunny terrace at Hotel Courcheneige. However, once the decision was taken to 'let her be free', as he put it, Peter was thrilled. Finally, he would learn to do those wide, graceful turns that his two sons executed in the deep powder, a manoeuvre he found very attractive but could not emulate. *There was not a better place to develop this skill*, he thought, *than with the famed Ecole de Ski Français.* He knew that powder skiing was dangerous but also forgiving and wonderful. 'Fear and freedom go together', he had told his sons.

Peter was better than an average recreational skier but still far below the competitive level. Probably at the age of 75, he already should have switched from downhill to cross country skiing. Last year his ski instructor had hinted that he might try a different sport, but Peter hated the idea of giving up the thrill of downhill skiing even though he knew he might very well break a bone in even a minor fall. He simply could not see himself plodding his way slowly along set cross-country tracks and missing out on the exhilaration of fast descents of downhill skiing.

Peter sarcastically mocked positive discussions about cross-country skiing at every opportunity. He would screw up his face and declare "Cross-country is no fun. It is boring. It is restrictive. With only the front of your boot attached to the skis, you are limited. In downhill, with the entire ski boot clamped on and secured by steel bindings, you are free to make your own path. It is fast and exhilarating. Downhill takes guts. It's not for wimps."

In his quest to be a legendary mountain skier (in his own mind, of course), he had taken many beginner and intermediate lessons, perfected the necessary pre-ski exercises, learnt the idiosyncrasies and etiquette of different chair, bubble, gondola and poma lifts, and even T-bars and rope tows. He had easily mastered the snowplough, stem christie, and even parallel skiing, though only on groomed runs. He knew that a top skier of his weight could burn up to 422 calories in an hour skiing. But none of this learning had yet enabled him to ski the difficult *couloirs* in deep snow or even ski the length of *Les Trois Vallées* with flair and confidence.

Realistically, he never hoped to make the top category of competitive downhill skiers, but he still prided himself on being adequately good. Already, he could go almost anywhere in the mountains in most snow conditions, and he still had his ambitions. He always put on his best face as he agonised to stretch, exercise, and dress, but this strain now took such a toll of his energy that he sometimes found he had little strength left for joining his ski class. He never admitted, even to himself, how much effort it now took just to put on his ski clothes; grunting, panting, sweating, and often perturbed by the wafts of stench steaming from his thermal underwear.

This morning Peter had felt a gnawing sense of urgency to get going, fearing that it might be now or never to make that final leap and powder ski in the style he wished. He had looked in the mirror, pulled up his stomach, looked as tall as he could and told himself, "I can do this!"

Now, he skied leisurely down the gentle green run from the Courcheneige to the centre of the station, casually stuffing his toque in his pocket to "give his head a chance" and tightening his antique boots on route. When he arrived at the appointed spot for his advanced class, he found the others were already there talking with the instructor. Gathered around Jacques Pelletier, the former French Olympic downhill champion, were nine other male skiers.

The first thing Peter noted was that his journalist friend Robert Arnett was already there; the second was that the participants were all considerably younger than he was. In fact, this was the first thing that he now noticed in every group. The youngest four men did not interest him at all. He knew they would be the fastest after the instructor. It was the others he had to concentrate on, as they would be his competitors in the middle and back of the pack during all the runs. Who were they? And more importantly – how well could they ski?

Jacques nodded and wasted no time when he saw Peter. "Fallow moi," he said in his best English, and the ten skiers leapt to begin their day exploring the deep powder of the Three Valleys. Practically running up the stairs, and brushing several beginners aside, Jacques elbowed his way to the front of the line and headed for the first bubble lift toward to the Saulire peak.

Puffing and sweating his way up the stairs, in the middle of the pack, Peter found himself having to take the second bubble. The humiliation had already begun.

As anticipated, the younger skiers were with the instructor and Peter was already in the rear with the more mature set. He plunged his parabolic skis into the side container, jumped into the second lift with feigned abandon, and sat down with five men whom he quickly calculated included his American friend, a Canadian he had seen at the Courcheneige, a Japanese and two others, probably Flemish-speaking Belgians or perhaps Russian louts. *It was difficult to tell what language that ghastly sound was*, he thought.

The most impeccably dressed was the relatively sober Japanese skier who looked vaguely familiar. The man said nothing all the way up the lift, but leant back and listened to the others go on chatting about themselves and Courchevel. With a start, Peter suddenly realised that this man was one of the trio he had overheard plotting at the Chabichou bar, and he suddenly felt a wave of panic. Happily, the man did not appear to recognise him. With some effort, Peter composed himself, smiled, and leant over to hug Robert Arnett, his American friend of many years.

After a warm exchange with Robert, Peter introduced himself to his neighbour, Jim Johnson, who announced himself to all as a Canadian. Peter had seen Jim with his two boys at the Courcheneige. The group conversation quickly turned to skiing, and after hearing their patter, Peter assured himself that he could keep up with Robert and Jim but he wasn't so sure about the tight-lipped Jap or the two quiet, scruffy, athletic looking strangers with wrap-around sunglasses. Their muscular builds vaguely reminded him of the famous photo of a bare-chested Russian Vladimir Putin astride a stallion.

Robert Arnett had arrived yesterday at the Méribel resort on the other side of the mountain. He had come by taxi from Geneva and was anxious to know what the conditions were like on the Courchevel side of the mountain where he preferred to ski. He was also looking forward to spending time with Peter.

Arnett was a well-known, retired CNN political reporter. He had met Peter in Courchevel on many previous occasions, but on this trip, he was stuck in Méribel because of his late decision to come skiing. He had been at Oxford University to receive an honorary degree for his critical coverage of various United States-led wars in the Middle East. It was an honour, but as an American, Robert had found the whole Oxford University affair in the Sheldonian Theatre much too formal and pretentious. It hadn't helped that he had forgotten to pack his black tie for the celebratory dinner, and was 'blackmailed' into paying the hotel concierge ten pounds to borrow a used one for the short occasion.

At the last minute, he had decided to get more out of the trip by joining Peter at Courchevel. Now he was on holiday and luxuriating in being free, far away from stuffy formality and dangerous war zones. For sure, skiing was more fun than stiff university events hosted by pretentious dons and privileged, overly clever students. *The Oxford interlude was almost as taxing as reporting on violence and war*, he thought; *a great ski and relaxed conversation with an old friend is just what I need.*

The former journalist was weary and still suffering from low level PTSD, or Post-Traumatic Stress Syndrome, a result of too many close encounters with so-called precision-guided US weapons, one of which had exploded near his hotel during his last assignment in Iraq. That had been the climax of too many other close calls. On this holiday, he did not want to hear about anyone else's problems. He'd had more than enough of his own!

"So, how are the conditions?" Robert queried Peter and his fellow classmates in his direct, assertive American way.

"Great!" responded Jim Johnson with the enthusiasm and vagueness that often characterised his countrymen abroad. The Canadian had already spent over a week skiing the red and blue runs on the few groomed *pistes* that were open during the storms, and he too was anxious "to get into the *hors-piste* powder".

"It's maybe not as good as Banff, Lake Louise or Whistler," Jim gently bragged after a few seconds' hesitation, "but not bad." He spoke with a notable western Canadian pride. Canadian to the core, Jim believed that everything about skiing in Alberta and British Columbia was marvellous. *Maybe he is right*, Peter thought as he watched him, *the Rockies are magnificent and maybe there is nothing sordid beneath the surface there...what you get is what you see, not here like in the more developed European Alps that are playgrounds of the global elite and international criminals!*

Robert listened to Jim with slight amusement. As an American he enjoyed the Canadian characteristic of pride yet modesty. He learnt later that Jim was an Albertan who worked in the Canadian Department of Global Affairs. Not a traditional diplomat, he had graduated with a BA in

Commerce from the University of Calgary. He, his wife Betty and their two young children were here in France for the year learning French. Jim was on a sabbatical for unilingual diplomats (of whom there were many from western Canada after a narrow Conservative victory in the last general election).

As might be expected of a Canadian, Jim was soft-spoken, kind, and competent. But, rarely consequential. He was having difficulty getting ahead in the diplomatic world, even in his growing field of military and terrorist security policies. Despite his high hopes for a superior civil service career, he was constantly being held back by his opinionated and archly feminist wife – a characteristic which grated on his Tory superiors.

His wife, on the other hand, had scaled the walls of academia as a feminist law professor, insisting that Jim do the lion's share of domestic work and raising their children. Even now during their French sabbatical, she was often back in Canada protecting her university turf, leaving Jim to care for their two boys. Jim was quietly relieved. She did not like sports and could not ski well, and last week she had been so pretentious around the Courcheneige ski lodge that he had heard the owner confiding to his staff that she must believe her abundant charms were enough to light up a room without even a match.

Jim was devoted to his boys, but being constantly tied down with a young family meant that he rarely could travel to exotic places on behalf of his government and therefore was unable to take the immediate and concrete actions necessary to advance his career. Although he was trained in anti-terrorism, he could not participate in military manoeuvres in foreign countries or visit the Middle East or South Asia to spy for his country. He was, however, anticipating a marvellous time with this ski group.

"How are you Brits finding it here?" Jim Johnson added after a brief silence.

Peter Worthington was up to the challenge. He explained how he had been coming to Courchevel for nearly thirty years and had practically raised his two boys on the slopes. The three men chatted for a while about the various runs and snow conditions. But it was a long ride, and Johnson and the two Slavic-looking skiers soon broke into an aggressive discussion in broken English about unruly children and dangerous snowboarders. Since his own children had left home and no longer came to Courchevel with him, Peter did not care much for the topic. He took the opportunity to lean close to Robert, turning his back to the Japanese man, and, while the others made small talk, he told him that they needed to talk about what he had overheard at the Chabichou bar the night before. Robert looked sceptical.

Peter expected Robert to be keen to know what happened but sceptical of any nefarious conclusions. His friend had always tended to distrust a news tip from any new source. In fact, Robert was not convinced about either the veracity or the implications of Peter's information, and gently reminded him with a grin that he was not in Courchevel for journalism or to ferret out a political intrigue, but to relax and rest. As the lift approached the station, however, he did promise Peter that they would talk more later. When the doors opened, they all moved quickly to the next lift – the huge cable car that had replaced the one that had violently careened down the mountain such a short time ago. The lift was eerily quiet as the skiers held onto the safety bars and peered down at the rocks below.

It was cold at the top of the mountain and the class began with a couple of warmup runs down the Mirabel side to get a feel for the conditions. It was exhilarating with powder snow and magnificent views but, on the return lifts, Peter Worthington was silent, preserving his strength and hiding his breathlessness. The happy chatter had begun to irritate him. He preferred to look out of the lift window at the few struggling skiers below, enjoying their odd tumbles and watching for the picturesque, weather-beaten mountain refuges that his sons used to call "Heidi huts".

Peter judged that he was doing fine, though he reckoned he would need time at the lunch break to recoup his forces for the afternoon session. He was secretly delighted when, on alighting, Jacques suggested they stop for a quick coffee at the restaurant on top of the Saulire while they could still snag a window table. That way he could give them some pointers before he presented them their first deep powder challenge.

The break was a great idea, and the view from the restaurant sitting on the edge of a cliff was indeed superb. Peter thought he could see the tip of Mount Blanc far in the distance. They were in full sun here at the top, but below them just a few metres down, clouds surrounded the peak with what looked to Peter like a thick, soft cotton batten mattress. It extended as far as the eye could see; only a few other peaks were visible in the distance. The thick large clouds looked so inviting that Peter had illusions of stretching out on them. The others barely seemed to notice, however. Jacques held forth with rules and stories about skiing and then his classmates competed to rehash their last daring runs on the Méribel side.

Peter listened. The break was far too short, he felt. He had barely loosened his boots and got to take only a few gasps of the winter air.

Finally, back outside, the group listened intently to their leader's last-minute instructions, then followed him on a path around the mountain peak stopping at the top of the Creux, a mammoth canyon with ungroomed, deep powder snow and more than a half a mile of moguls. After leading the way down a narrow path and then making a very short stop to watch and account for his class, Jacques told the skiers to follow directly on his path down the next run.

"Keep up and don't go wandering off across the mountain!" He yelled back, "You're not wimps."

Instead of following the marked trail, Jacques hopped up at a right angle and barrelled full steam directly down the face of the mountain. His body sank in snow up to his knees but somehow his tips seemed to pop up again and again. He turned adroitly and rhythmically in the deep snow, knees flexed and body forward until he arrived with a flourish at the bottom. The others watched intently and then followed one at a time. Peter's rivals, the two strangers and the Japanese, had no trouble. Then Jim Johnson, followed by Robert Arnett, finished the run with difficulty but both still arrived intact.

Peter was last. He had to stop several times during the descent and barely made it to the waiting group. When he arrived, he was out of breath, his legs were trembling, and it crossed his mind that he might have a heart attack. Arnett did not want to embarrass him but was alarmed at the prospect of his friend going into convulsions and dying right there on the spot. Jacques laughed and scolded Peter for not following his moves. "Smarter up. Next time, stay closer," he exclaimed with a grin.

Peter gamely pulled himself together and managed to follow the group down the next steep run, then around the bottom part of the mountain where he chose to leave them and let them continue their lesson without him. He took a lift directly back to the Courcheneige hotel, arrived panting and exhausted, and went right to the bar for a drink.

Sue, just out of her low intermediate class, was already there with a friend and met him with a surprised smile. "What went wrong? Couldn't you keep it up?" she joked. Peter was insulted and hurt. Smarting, he took his drink to a corner where he sat by himself, thinking philosophically about freedom and the glory of skiing.

I really think that skiers live in a dream world, he reflected sulkily to himself. *They come to life on the slopes and imagine themselves as finally released from the restraints of work, society and family, but they are not really free at all. Skiers may dream they are in a perfect world, but they are actually part of a social hierarchy that controls where and how they ski.*

Peter understood that skiers are constrained to showing their athletic prowess on manmade runs, designated by colour. Green for beginners, blue for intermediates, red for advanced intermediates, and black and double diamond for experts. Some freedom. A few adventurous highfliers dare to ski *hors-piste* or on runs that have not been groomed, but even they are barred from the dangerous craggy areas of ravines and boulders that are impossible for security officials to monitor.

The social distinctions among skiers are even greater than that categorisation, he mused. *Each class of skier has its own rules and boundaries*. Peter had often told his sons that freedom does not mean unconfined movement. A philosopher might argue that there IS no freedom in skiing; rules, both explicit and implicit, must be obeyed. Ability and social conventions reserve the edges of the regular runs for the best skiers to cruise straight down. Less capable skiers can only maintain control by traversing the centre terrain from one side to the other side of the slope. The weakest skiers have to accept the humiliation of snowploughing slowly back and forth across the runs, while the somewhat better skiers cut behind and even in front of them with abandon, demonstrating a clear show of social distinction.

Then, Peter thought glumly, *there are the snowboarders who endanger us all. They make up their own rules as they go.*

"Ah youth! Pass the bottle!" Peter murmured to himself, reciting the author, Joseph Conrad.

Peter reasoned that skiers by nature are searching for freedom and glory but they cannot escape their essentially conservative natures. They tend to accept the latest convention or conformity. *The reality*, he thought, *is that skiing, like most other social activity, is devoid of real choice. Skiers may think they have some individual purpose in their activities, but they are governed by rules and conventions based on familiar patterns and hierarchies. They are not any freer than a chess player, who moves individual pieces by choice but always within a particular set of traditions and conditions.*

Peter was now lost in his own philosophical thoughts. What is the meaning of freedom when behaviour is directed and controlled from sunrise to sunset? The smallest changes in the rules upset skiers. When runs are closed for grooming or because of accidents or poor conditions, skiers are offended and upset, almost beyond belief. They complain, "How could they do this?", "I waited all day", "It's the only way back to our chalet!" and so on.

Even the slightest change in snow conditions upsets beginners and experts alike, and they always blame it for their bad performance. Each type of snow is analysed to death and calls for slogans such as "The runs are powdery", "No, they are icy with only light snow on top of ice", "No, it is just hard pack", "You will find fresh snow at the top and corn snow at the bottom" or "You are all wrong, the snow differs from run to run".

Still stinging from Sue's less than flattering observation, Peter stopped daydreaming about freedom and conformity, pulled on his jacket and headed out by foot to the British pub in the village where he was to meet his friend Robert. He was anxious to discuss the terrible implications of what he had heard in the Chabichou bar.

He and Robert had been skiing friends for years. They had met here in Courchevel years ago and had kept in close contact. The pair made a startling contrast, and not just because of their age. Peter was a very straightforward guy. There was nothing complex or hidden about him. He considered himself to be a typical Englishman. Self-reliant, he had worked his way up from a working-class background and attended school only till he was 16, stopping well before he could attain his A-levels. Through native intelligence, curiosity, perseverance and hard work, however, he eventually had become the owner of several small construction companies in and around London and learnt the intricacies of business finance.

Peter's confidence and ability were evident in his management style which could be called "very easy going". That did not mean that he was a fool. He hired every competent immigrant from the European Union he could, paying the lowest wages possible under the British law. But he treated all foreigners with respect and fairness. He even became close friends with many of them and their families and helped them in myriad ways.

Peter lived with his wife in one of the loveliest villages of Oxfordshire and commuted by train into the city every day, except of course when he took his family skiing in France – which was every opportunity he could get. He and Sue took many short trips to Courchevel, but the longest holidays were generally limited to the Christmas season and occasionally the early Easter period.

Peter's ready smile and joviality contrasted with the sombre personality of Robert Arnett. Rob, as only his closest friends knew him, was from a lower-class American family. He had been brought up in Raleigh, North Carolina in a home characterised best by grinding poverty and self-loathing. His father had left in 1944, ostensibly to fight in World War II, but actually to escape family responsibilities after the birth of three children. He never returned after the war but found another woman and started a new family.

Robert's mother, only 21 years old when she was abandoned, found herself in desperate straits with no education or means of support. On several occasions, the welfare agencies had tried to take the children and put them in foster care, but she fought tenaciously and successfully and kept her kids at home.

As the firstborn, Robert's mom had protected him as much as she could despite the circumstances. She relied on him in myriad ways and he matured quickly, but his emotional scars were permanent. As a very small boy, he developed an inward-looking personality and discipline that served him well throughout his life. He was an excellent athlete but a mediocre student, barely scraping into college, where he hoped to play varsity football and basketball. His mindset of extreme expediency and love of sports gave him the will to excel, but his small frame prevented him from star status on the court or gridiron.

In his sophomore year, Robert had transferred from a community college to Duke University where he became an avid history student, eventually becoming a Rhodes Scholar at Pembroke College, Oxford. He completed a PPE degree with a good upper second-class standing, like most Americans who went there for a second BA. After graduation, the young student returned to his home state of North Carolina. His early years back in the US were difficult. He considered entering politics but unlike his role model, Bill Clinton, he possessed neither the superficiality nor the personality to do well in the field. He had developed a strong moral compass, and, like many men of his generation, was committed to justice and truth and felt a strong need to put his ideals into action.

Robert's first choice had been to teach in a college or university, but after a very short time back in the United States he switched to journalism, an honourable profession at the time. It was clear to him that academia was the unique preserve of those with an Ivy League or Oxbridge doctorate. While he was undoubtedly brilliant and well disciplined, work in higher education was out of the question. He had developed a characteristic common among American Oxford-men of his generation. He was confused about where and whether he fit into the upper echelons of society, and soon developed a high degree of cynical and tough-minded realism alongside a set of confused norms; he abhorred enclaves of privilege and coveted them at the same time.

After a period of moping and freelancing, Arnett had landed a job as a television reporter for CNN. His realist mindset was perfect for the job. He travelled the world and often broke leading stories about international relations and the world's greatest statesmen and scoundrels. It was an exciting life, and he found he loved to live on the edge. He enjoyed witnessing the messiest conflicts of the century and served in nearly every American war as a combat journalist. His work put him in harrowing circumstances, often embedded with the US Army. He was proud to associate with TV stars like Anderson Cooper, Nic Robertson and Wolf Blitzer.

For twenty years, he had enjoyed a very successful marriage, and when he wasn't abroad lived quietly with his wife, Marjory, and son, Charles, in Bethesda, Maryland. Then his life fell apart. Several horrific military engagements and near-death incidents in Iraq, Afghanistan, and Syria left him shell-shocked. He was ill, tired and depressed. His faith in humanity faltered, and his certainty of right and wrong blurred. His nerves finally snapped and he gave in to treatment for post-traumatic stress.

Robert was still in treatment when his wife received a cancer diagnosis, and at the same time, he discovered his 20-year-old son, who had followed him to Duke University, was heavily into hard drugs. Without warning, the boy permanently divorced himself from the family. When Robert was finally released from his treatment at a military hospital, he returned to help Marjory, but her cancer quickly advanced to stage-four and she died within a few months. He could not find his son. He was once more shattered emotionally.

Blaming himself and his long absences for his family's misfortunes, he vowed he would never go on another foreign reportage. It was not a difficult choice. It was an emotional relief. He had already begun to think that US policies in the Central Asia, the Middle East and elsewhere always began in idealism but ended in turmoil. *War*, he thought, *was not the force that gave America its meaning. It was repulsive*!

Robert had already begun to have deep reservations about where modern journalism was headed. It was less fact based, more emotional, opinionated and biased than it used to be. He could agree that the Internet was more immediate than his old-style reporting, drew huge audiences and had unlimited processing power. But it was unbearably shallow and television news was mimicking it. The thirst for factual and emotional knowledge was mistakenly replacing wisdom.

Overall, he detested social media and perceived it as a step backwards. Twitter and Facebook especially encouraged people to hold onto their biases and adhere to uninformed viewpoints. Twitter allowed no room to make intelligent, thoughtful arguments, seek compromise or show respect for opposing ideas. It relied on bombast, ad homonyms and vacuous certainty to denigrate other viewpoints, not logic.

They were popular forums because they were easy and unvetted. Any dolt could be an expert. It was simply a way to join up with likeminded thinkers and throw stones at all who disagreed. They were good for letting off steam but misleading, short-sighted and dishonest. Social media's overall contribution, he concluded, was negative and divisive. Fake news was on the rise.

Robert had been ready to build a new life at home. However, when he sought to change the nature of his job, CNN fired him for lack of focus and inability to keep up with the times. He went on a drinking binge that spiralled out of control and only ended several months later, when he got the letter from Oxford saying he was to be awarded an honorary DLitt for his service to journalism. The unexpected notice of the award had cheered him immensely and helped him pull himself together. He decided to go to Oxford and when he heard about it Peter had convinced him to use the stipend to ski once again in Courchevel where their families had spent many memorable holidays in the past. Last night, when he had finally arrived, he was slightly annoyed to receive a message from Peter fussing about some incident in a bar. All he wanted was to relax and lose himself in some thrilling skiing,

Peter had arranged to meet Robert in the English Bar, one of the most popular gathering places in the centre of the ski resort. The beer and food in the bar were superb and the warm atmosphere attracted English-speaking people from all over the area. Robert came directly from his ski class to absorb some of the social action before Peter got there. There were a lot of good-looking women on the prowl. He wasn't quite ready to engage yet, but he enjoyed looking.

Now, as he watched Peter approach, he checked out his old friend and decided he was none the worse for his ski day, though he did look a bit agitated. They embraced and commented lightly about their ski class. Then, looking around the darkened room, Peter suddenly was nervous. He manoeuvred his friend to the closest private corner, but the bar was crowded and loud, and there always seemed to be someone observing them and listening to their conversation. It was unnerving.

Peter tried to keep what he had to say as clear and concise as possible. He had overheard three men conversing in the Chabichou bar. He gathered that they were implicated in a scheme to drive the hotels and shops in the area to financial ruin.

"Hold on! They are not the problem. It's not them," Robert interjected incredulously. "The financial turndown is due to a combination of a downturn in the global economy and the lousy weather. Perhaps global warming."

"No," Peter retorted, "it's more than that. Those men were gloating about the role they had played in raising fear in the area. I believe they caused unusual, unexplained accidents, and even deaths. They even hinted that terrorism might be involved."

Robert examined his friend warily. He was aware that the confluence of bad news in the region was being reported in the business sections of national radio and television programs in France. It was sometimes even discussed in the context of ISIS attacks across Europe, but he thought all this was very farfetched.

"One hotel, the Rond-Point des Pistes has already declared bankruptcy and is up for sale for a pittance of its value," Peter said glumly. "And, there are rumours that several more could be on the market soon. These aren't just any hotels but some of the leading holiday venues in France and Europe, the pride of the country. They embody the finest in French tradition, culture and cuisine."

Then, in his enthusiasm for the story, Peter took his eye off the ball and got carried away with details. "The hotels," he said, "include spacious suites with amazing 360-degree views, 180 degrees, 90 degrees, pocket views and no views. To survive this downturn, all the resorts need the same things – abundant snow, a calm atmosphere, a stable economy and strong euro, and no more accidents or bad publicity to frighten clients away."

Robert was tired and getting irritated. "Please, get to the point Peter. So, these three guys are happy that things are bad. I'm against injustice as much as anyone, but what is the plot?"

Peter lost his cool and practically shouted at him, "Don't you get it? The French government, fraudulent businessmen, and the Russian mafia are here in Courchevel conspiring to sabotage the ski resort as part of their plan to buy up the best of the Savoie. I am convinced they are doing everything they can – even murdering people – to frighten tourists and ruin businesses so they can get a cheap deal."

Robert stared at Peter with disbelief. "Total nonsense!" he exclaimed. "Buy up all the best real estate in the Savoie? Ridiculous, Peter. It would take billions of euros, and if the French public ever got wind of a possible wholesale buyout of their heritage, the idea would be quashed immediately."

"But not if the deal were kept hush-hush," Peter objected quietly after a furtive glance around the room. "It would be a *fait accompli*. In global business, it all depends on whose pocket you line. Of course, the price must be right. For that the owners must be shit frightened that more bad publicity will drive even more clients away. And we know they can't hold on much longer. The euro is expected to continue to decline, and from what I have seen, the Russians are prepared to support the deal with dirty money that is being laundered through international business and banking. Don't forget that this is the largest ski area in the world. Courchevel 1850 is the Russians' favourite skiing centre because of its exclusivity and location near Geneva, a great financial capital. Putin is even alleged to own a *dacha* here."

"Preposterous. They would need the support of the French government to pull off such a scheme."

"The problem with you, Robert, is that you know everything about international journalism and nothing about global business" Peter retorted. "Organised crime has evolved in the post-Cold War world. Corrupt businessmen and high government officials have merged into global criminal networks. The end of the Cold War, the deregulation of capital movements, and the development of the Internet have led to both qualitative and quantitative growth in international criminality. When it is in their interest, some police, mafia and even terrorists join the corruption. In this case, with President Marchand and his Minister of the Interior onside, the bad guys and their friend Vladimir Putin are sure to make a bundle in kickback money. I think the deal is all but done."

When Robert did not respond, Peter continued. "Let me explain how these things work in simple terms. First, you have to understand that after the USSR fell and primitive capitalism took hold in that country, many Russians became very rich in fields such as energy and real estate. There are an estimated

10000 to 20000 of these people who now form a kind of oligarchy – some would say kakistocracy – in the country. Second, many of these rich people – you can call them kleptocrats, businessmen, financiers, or crooks, whatever you prefer – need to hide their illicit gains and get their dirty money out of the country. Their actions may be motivated by honest business activities, but more likely by criminal activity such as tax evasion or money laundering. Whatever the reason, these rich businessmen want to store their money in western banks and invest in luxury real estate in safe western economies."

Peter glanced around the bar before he launched into an explanation of a number of complicated techniques for evading government controls that he had learnt from his London experiences. "In Russia, most of the large businesses are state-owned corporations, virtual branches of government. The easiest way for them to get money out of Russia is to use a standard government bank. This is carried out on a daily basis by legitimate businesses, or at least by those acceptable to the government."

He paused. "In Moscow, for example, they can send money overseas through a Russian-owned entity such as Gazprombank. But this only works if the government is in agreement with the deal or is in alliance with the companies' leaders. For others, a state-controlled oil company such as Rosneft, or a large private business close to the government, and run, say, by a Russian billionaire, can use companies such as UC Rusal (an aluminium producer), EuroSibEnergo (a large hydroelectric producer) or GAZGroup (an automotive company) to carry it off. These companies are mostly run by Putin's cronies or former KGB men, like Putin, himself. They would have no problem with the bank or the government, would they?"

Robert looked sceptical as he sipped his beer, so Peter piled it on thicker. "Another method they use is to first send the money, for example, to Chechnya or Moldova. The Russian government often awards companies in these areas with large Russian construction projects like building roads or bridges. The companies earn billions of dollars in government contracts and then their corrupt managers have to get the money out of the country or lose it through taxation. They sometimes place it in regional banks that can hold it overseas in a foreign currency. This is the Wild East after all."

At this point two laughing young women approached them but Peter glared and dismissed them with a wave of his hand.

He continued: "Rich Russians and others, who don't have government approval, have more discreet methods of stashing their stolen to get their private fortunes or stolen wealth offshore. Cyprus, Geneva and New York are obvious destinations. I see it all the time in London. Historically, funds have been invested in assets such as property – iconic businesses such as the Chelsea Football Club and apartment complexes in Northern Cyprus, skyscrapers in NY and high-end real estate in London – and now they want to expand to owning property such as luxurious ski resorts in safe and secure places like Courchevel."

Robert said nothing. He did not need a lecture on economics. On the other hand, he had heard rumours about Russian thugs landing in Geneva with suitcases full of cash, though he had not given them much credence.

"Robert, if you believe those methods are too crude," Peter went on with a sigh, "there also are indirect methods to achieve the same goal. A popular way to move funds overseas and escape the prying eyes of government tax collectors is called 'mirror trading'."

Peter looked intently at Robert who evidently had not heard of this simple approach. "A Russian broker, for example, calls the equities desk at, say, the Deutsche Bank Moscow headquarters and places two trades simultaneously...in the first, he uses Russian rubbles to buy blue chip Russian stock, in the second trade, perhaps acting with the same company, probably offshore in another country – such as the British Virgin Islands or London or Geneva – he sells the newly acquired Russian stock in exchange for stocks in a foreign currency – dollars, pounds or euros. In other words, he buys stock and then sells it, not to make a profit, but to expatriate the money. This manoeuvre turns currency that is stuck in one country into another currency outside the country."

"That is illegal, surely," Robert interjected.

"No. Mirror trading is not illegal because it does not contravene government financial regulations and the capital flows may never appear in the balance of payments statistics. But is it improper? Unethical? You bet. Billions of rubbles are spirited out of Russia in this way. Putin and his friends have accumulated fortunes in foreign currencies using this method."

"For Christ's sake!" Robert exclaimed as he noticed another group of young women in the bar watching them and listening a little too closely to their conversation. They weren't flirting. "That is enough. I think you are paranoid.

Stuff like this ends up in bloodshed. This is making me jumpy. Let's wrap it up. I've got to get back. I'll see you at Ski School tomorrow. Let me think about it. It all sounds pretty farfetched. We'll decide then if there is anything we could or should do."

Peter was irritated that Robert would not take his theory about a major plot seriously. He felt sure he was on to something that was terrifying. He waved goodbye, then walked slowly back up the ski slope to the Courcheneige hotel. After a rather glum dinner with his wife, he headed back down to the Lana bar for a few nightcaps. It had been a long, aggravating day.

Chapter 5
Bloody Murder on the
Terrace: Hotel Courcheneige

Early the next morning, while enjoying their *café au lait* and *croissants*, two dozen clients in the Courcheneige restaurant collectively gasped in horror. The serenity of the magnificent, snowy scene in front of them was shattered by an unbelievable sight. Part of a man's bloody arm blasted out the nozzle of the huge snow machine and flew across the terrace towards the folded blue canvas chairs in front of their window. It landed silently in the fresh snow, all sound drowned out by the whining motor and the grating noise of the machine's wheels on the wooden deck.

The machine continued to emit fragments of flesh and red wool through the freezing air, but before Gilles, the young operator, could ram the gear forward to the full stop position, it choked and stalled. Clogging the blades was a man's body, still largely submerged in the snow. The jaws of the sharp blade were clamped hungrily on the right shoulder. Under the body, the snow was stained bright red; the man's eyes stared blankly towards the heavens and his mouth was open as if uttering a silent cry for help.

Nothing could have prepared the guests or staff at the intimate, family-run hotel in the French Alps for this gory, early-morning horror. The fashionably dressed early risers dropped their *croissants* and fell into a stunned silence. For a few horrible seconds, no one moved. One of them commented afterwards that those few seconds seemed like an hour, that time ticked slower than the clock. Time, of course, is an illusion. The notion of time as an independent, measurable linear quantity is ludicrous, as Einstein proved with his theory of time and space, but that was not what the observers were thinking about.

All eyes were riveted on the body protruding from the mouth of the yellow, blood-splattered snow blower and on the mangled limb, that had dropped beside it. Standing over the cold cadaver, Gilles was in shock. Suddenly Jim Johnson, seated in the corner window with his boys, recognised his new friend from the ski class. He uttered a cry, bolted onto the terrace, and fell to his knees beside the body. "Peter!" he screamed. "My God, Peter!" The spell was broken, and within seconds, Gilles and several other onlookers were working to dislodge the man's arm and shoulder from the blades.

The dead man was indeed Peter Worthington. Peter was well-known to the regular hotel guests as a charming British real-estate broker from London. He was liked by all in the hotel – staff and guests alike. Friendly and outgoing, with his bald head and ruddy face framed by an unruly fringe of white hair, Peter was a familiar sight in the restaurant and bar. In the years he had been coming to this small hotel, he had built a reputation as a lover of gourmet food and drink, honesty, good humour and friendship. His booming laugh was a trademark as was his sense of fun on and off the slopes.

It was with shock and supreme disbelief that fellow-guest Jim Johnson and the others now regarded the body. Peter was dressed as he had been the evening before when he had said goodbye to his wife and left for the kilometre walk down the gentle ski-run to the village. His open ski jacket with the Three Valley pass on the remaining sleeve revealed his red wool sweater and black ski pants. As usual, his head was bare "to give it a chance". But the animated smile and the sparkle in his eyes had been extinguished.

Tentatively, Jim tried to close the staring eyes and demanded calmly, in almost fluent French, that Gilles fetch his father, the owner, and call the police. The lanky, good-looking young Frenchman quickly vanished and in minutes returned with his father. Pierre Heuilly was pale and obviously horrified. When he had taken in the scene, he turned calmly to Jim. "We can't leave him here to terrify our guests. An avalanche last night blocked all traffic coming up the mountain. Help won't get up here for hours," he said. Then he looked again at the body, shook his head, and told Gilles to call the village police and the medical centre. "Tell them we will have to take the body down on the sleigh."

"Where is Mrs Worthington?" Jim asked.

Nobody responded so Jim quietly volunteered to find her. As a new friend of the Worthingtons, he felt responsible, though he cringed at the thought of facing the frail, attractive woman and bringing her to the scene. Jim disappeared into the hotel. By the time he returned with Sue, the body, together with fragments of its dismembered arm, had already been bundled onto a ski-rescue sleigh and Gilles and his father had taken some photos, wrapped Peter's body in blankets and were strapping it securely on the sleigh.

As the two stepped out into the cold morning air, Sue clutched Jim's arm as if to steady herself, but she said nothing as her eyes took in the scene. Then, with characteristic calm she approached the sled, knelt beside it and reached out to touch her husband's cold face. When she looked up, her eyes were full of tears and her pale face was distorted by pain.

"He was such a wonderful man. What happened?" she asked softly. "I don't understand what is going on. What happened?"

Pierre Heuilly responded in broken English, gesturing with his hands to describe how Gilles had uncovered the body when he had begun to clear the terrace after the heavy snowfall from the previous evening. Large flakes of snow, which continued to fall, had already tempered and disguised some of the horror of the bloody discovery with a soft layer of pristine white.

Sue's blurry eyes focused on Jim.

"He didn't come back last night," she said, "I waited up, but he didn't come back. I should have gone looking for him, but I fell asleep. He must have had a heart attack after his walk up from the village."

Jim did not contradict her; there was time enough for her to learn that violence and murder were involved; that the pool of blood he had seen beneath the body had come from a bullet wound inflicted by someone who wanted to kill Peter. Instead he glanced at Pierre and Gilles for support and confirmation before responding.

"We're going to take him down to the medical centre behind the Croisette, Sue. The roads are blocked, so we'll use the snowmobile to take him down on the sled. The doctor will be able to tell us what happened."

"I'm coming," she said with emotion. "Wait for me, while I change."

Ten minutes later, they made a strange sight, winding slowly down the gentle Bellecôte ski run toward the village. Sue, in her florescent pink ski suit, was the most visible in the near white-out as she wrapped her arms around Gilles on the back of the large skidoo; her husband's body bounced along on the sleigh behind, followed by Jim and Pierre on skis.

Gilles was the first to enter the *cabinet de médecine* where a young, tired-looking doctor awaited. With characteristic impetuousness, Gilles rushed to explain how he had come upon the body, but he was quite incoherent and nervous as he tried to make it clear that it was not his fault. "I always clean off the terrace before noon so that it will be ready for lunch drinks, but..."

The doctor brushed past Gilles and held the door for Pierre and Jim who were struggling to bring in the body. Dr Daniel LeBlanc, whose ironic name reminded everyone of a Charles Dickens' character, was a specialist in back and shoulder injuries, but every ski season he looked after breaks and sprains of all descriptions. Normally, within days of the first snowfall, his waiting room was full of patients. This week a trickle had already begun. However, he hadn't expected anyone this early in the morning, and it was only by chance that the call from the hotel had found him in the clinic, as normally he skied until lunch unless he was paged.

The young doctor supervised the deposition of the body in his surgery and exchanged a few words with Pierre before closing the door and making a cursory examination. When he emerged a few moments later, he approached Sue who sat in shock and tears, being awkwardly comforted by Jim. He offered her a glass of water and two small pills from a plastic container.

"This will help you through the next few hours," he said softly. "The village police will be here as soon as they can." Then, as Sue looked up at him quizzically, he added, "As far as I can tell, Mrs Worthington, your husband died of a bullet wound."

Sue said nothing but wandered numbly into the surgery and embraced the body of her late husband. She was shaking and her face was wet with tears. Practical to the core, however, she fumbled through his trousers, looking for his wallet and the keys to their car. She still had not found them when the local *gendarme* arrived in his sharp blue uniform with gold buttons and flat kepi. He was only a low-level functionary in the Ministry of the Interior, a former school friend of Gilles, but nevertheless he wanted everyone to understand his importance.

"What are you doing? Why have you taken the body from the scene of the crime?" he enquired rudely of Sue. His small handlebar moustache hid the fact that he was far too young and inexperienced to be handling a complicated murder case. It gave him a comic air. He prodded again. "Madame, don't touch the body. Why did you bring the body down here?" Pat could not, or would not, respond. Her French had never been very strong, and, grief stricken, she could not even hear the French, let alone know how to answer in a foreign language.

Gilles couldn't contain himself. "We thought he might still be alive, you idiot. The main roads are blocked. It will take hours to get help up at the hotel. The overnight storm has caused a loss of electricity nearly everywhere and it is difficult to get phone calls and messages through. Grow up. Can't you see the woman is beside herself? It's her husband. He's been shot. He's dead."

The young *gendarme* ignored his former classmate and proceeded to whisper first with the doctor, then Jim. From their responses, he tried to piece together the outline of the story so he could relay it to his superiors. It appeared Mr Worthington had gone down to the station the previous night to have a drink. His friend thought he had been weary and depressed by the ski school. But that was as much as the *gendarme* could get from him.

Sue sat in shock. She confirmed that Peter had come back early from his ski class, had an early dinner, and departed shortly afterwards to go down to the bar at the Lana hotel where he often hung out with friends and liked the way the bartender mixed his drinks. She was tired and had gone to bed not knowing where her husband was. But her worst worry at the time was that he would have too big a hangover to ski the next day, not that he would be dead.

If she had gone with Peter to the village two days earlier, she would have known what he had overheard at the Chabichou bar. As it was, she knew nothing about the plot or what her husband had divulged to Robert Arnett. She had only a vague premonition when he said goodbye last night that something was wrong. She thought it must have been his skiing, or maybe the bad weather. Now, she was very upset and confused. She withdrew from the group to call her family in Oxfordshire to break the horrible news and let them help her make arrangements to take Peter's body back to England for burial when it was released. She wanted to escape the resort as soon as possible.

Later that morning, at ten o'clock, ski classes convened at the Croisette as usual, though few runs were open after the heavy snowfall.

Already news of Peter's murder had spread. When Robert Arnett heard that Peter had been murdered, he was incredulous, deeply shaken, and his thoughts immediately went back to the conspiracy theory. Only he had been privy to Peter's thoughts and his friend's concerns had sounded absurd at the time. There was nothing worse than innocent people dying for other people's causes and the thought made Robert furious.

He was not the only one to speculate about the motives for the murder. When the young *gendarme* reported the crime to his senior officers in the nearby city of Albertville, they were shocked and appalled at news of yet another death in the ski village. They feared this might be enough to send the village and region into fear, and perhaps, chaos. What was going on?

As news of Peter's death spread through the area, conjecture and rumour soon enveloped the mountain villages. A sense of helplessness and fear spread quickly. The concept of Courchevel as an inviolable sanctuary disappeared. The usual *schadenfreude* culture of a ski resort, where people always seem to experience joy at other peoples' misfortune quickly disappeared. Everyone knew they should not spread rumours about the murder but they did anyway. Repeating gossip seemed to hold the society together. Public nervousness escalated to fear and even dread as the rumours grew ever wilder and spread rapidly through the region and eventually into metropolitan France and beyond. Within hours, through word of mouth and social media, the very name Courchevel 1850 became associated with death and murder.

The deeply mysterious and horrific events of the past month, culminating now in Peter's death, created the appearance of intrigue and proof of a political crime. The Albertville police relayed details of the murder to Paris and immediately the small-town media was inundated with calls from national radio and television reporters. Gory stories about the ski resort went viral. Both the yellow press and the Internet screamed headlines about *Ski terrorism in Courchevel*, panicking people who were looking to purchase condos and homes there. No one was certain what was true and what was *fake news*. Within hours anxious buyers, already spooked, had reconsidered and begun to withdraw their down payments. Some potential tourists and skiers cancelled their reservations, and skiers currently in the hotels and condos felt terrified and imprisoned by the rumours of violence and terrorism. Overcome by fear, some of them simply decided to stay indoors to avoid potentially difficult people and nefarious events while others left the area.

Chapter 6
Global Conspirators
L'Annapurna

The Annapurna hotel below the altiport is a grand edifice named after a mountain in the Himalayas. It is reputed by many to be one of the finest resorts in France, indeed in the world, and it was here that Inoyne Watanabe headed after his ski class on Monday. He took the poma lift up past the Courcheneige hotel so he could ski leisurely down past the altiport to the back door of the Annapurna.

Watanabe sat down for a few minutes outside the hotel, trying to get his breath before the high-level meeting. He was pleased with how things were progressing. He recalled their founding meeting a couple of years ago at restaurant Chez Paul on the Place Dauphine, just off the Quai des Orfèvres on the Île de la Cité in Paris. The group included himself, Lionel Jospin and Baron de Rothschild. Sometimes they invited specialists such as suicide terrorists or counterfeit specialists, but none were ever invited twice.

Unlike earlier criminals of the Cold War era, they were not spies or communist revolutionaries, or anarchists.

Their triumvirate was characterised only by greed. They were experts in how to help the rich move their money around the world and how to profit from it.

Watanabe was proud of their methods. They were extremely careful about where they met and how they communicated. They met in exclusive, discreet restaurants. They knew that American and British security agencies were tracking foreign email and criminal messages on the Internet, so when they had to send an urgent message, they used a technique known among spies as *foldering* that is the equivalent of a deep drop used by spies and spy writers during the Cold War. They would write their emails to each other but then not send them. They possessed a copy of the password to get into each other's computers where they could read the messages which were never sent and thus not available to anyone who monitored the Internet.

It had taken three years for them to come up with their master plan to get control of the entire skiing industry in Courchevel. Albertville and Courchevel had recently hosted a spectacular Winter Olympics. The area was perfect or their grand plot and was ripe for a take-over.

The group had launched their plan at a place known for both high quality cuisine and its distance from the cosmopolitan onlookers and police. The restaurant, St Sulplice, was at 2000 metres, the highest stop in the Three Valleys and the cuisine was world-class. Its owner, Jean Sulpice, had won a two-star Michelin award at the childish age of 26 and had never looked back. The food was both brilliantly traditional and modern and guests were welcomed in smart casual clothes or ski togs.

Watanabe, like his associates, had skied the 15 miles to Val Torrens that morning, arriving just in time for lunch. He could remember it in vivid detail. The Minister of the Interior had entered by the side door, the other two from the front.

"Salut," Jospin had called to the head waiter he had known for years. "What's the best steak you have today?"

Jean smiled and replied, "Filet Mignon, for you, boss."

"Okay, let's have it. Rare. The others show up?"

"Yep, they are on the terrace. They just got here."

Baron de Rothschild, dressed like the dandy businessman he was, stood up to welcome the minister as he approached. With a wide smile he delivered an exaggerated *bonjour monsieur le minister.* followed by a slight bow to show his fealty. Watanabe also stood up as tall as his five feet two would allow and held out his hand for a proper handshake "Bonjour Jacques. It is great to see you again."

They took their places and ordered Compari and Orange before getting down to business. "Well, who are we seeing today?" Minister Jospin asked abruptly.

The Baron answered in a much lower voice. "The leader of the mafia in Paris is coming to explain how he and his accomplices intend to play their roles in Courchevel."

"We must ensure that they don't get out of hand. We need to frighten people, not murder them. We don't want police called in," Watanabe had chipped in.

"Right on, Watanabe. We want to make a profit, not start a war," the minister replied with a smile. "We don't want a lot of bad publicity when the President visits us in Courchevel."

Watanabe could see their guest – approaching. Yuri, the muscular Russian mafia leader was neatly dressed and appeared to be on his rare best behaviour. Clearly, he was aware that these three gentlemen (as he sarcastically thought of them) could determine how much money he made in this trip to the Alps.

Watanabe didn't like Yuri, and as soon as their guest was seated and had ordered he got straight to the point. "Your job was to scare people. Not kill them," he bluntly told the mafia leader as the others ogled the steaks that were arriving for another table.

"Nah. We won't. We had to deal with some emergencies. Everything is fine. The local police have still not discovered why the big lift went down. And, oh yeah, we have hired two females to help us with the logistics. They are Muslim Americans coming from Syria and Paris so there should be no trace to us here. They are good-looking. They will be useful."

At this point, de Rothschild had made one of his typically facetious remarks.

"We all understand that in Shakespeare's time men played women's roles, and that today, in the age of feminism, women play both men's and women's roles. But let's get serious. How many men do you have to counter any serious issues we might encounter? We need to assure the President that everything is okay.".

Before Watanabe could replay the rest of the conversation in his mind, his colleagues started to arrive at the hotel.

As he took off his ski boots and pulled his shoes from his backpack, Watanabe checked out every detail of the fantastic hotel. The boot-room boasted individual lockers made of carved blond wood and a large mirror in which all the ladies and girls, of whichever gender, could prim themselves before hitting the slopes. As he stood there, two smiling transvestites deep in conversation came arm-in-arm out of the ladies' room.

He also noticed a large swimming pool behind a glass wall, and his eyes lingered on the beautiful women lounging on its deck. Wandering past the pool, he found the bar and then crossed slowly to the restaurant where his co-conspirators had agreed to meet.

On the way, Watanabe couldn't help having some misgivings that the whole enterprise they had embarked upon was perhaps more 'flummadiddle' than anything. He liked that new, cool word. He had just learnt that it meant foolish or worthless. A fleeting smile flickered across his inscrutable Japanese face. He was pleased with himself.

Watanabe passed leisurely through the elegant, popular, and somewhat gaudy bar. Plush black leather sofas hugged the red-orange carpet behind huge coffee tables, each made of half a mahogany tree trunk. In the corner, he noticed a Yamaha grand piano topped by a silver encased elephant tusk. The ceiling was at least twenty-five feet high and made of highly polished, curved mahogany timber that ran from the cathedral windows along the bar and then into the main dining room. The red-orange of the carpet complimented the mahogany wood in the coffee tables and ceiling and imparted vibes of warmth and vivacity.

The sombre black furnishings of the Omar Sharif bar offered a sharp contrast with the stupendous, bright alpine panorama from the large windows looking out towards the Saulire. Nestled on the brilliant mountain side well below the peak was the altiport, where Watanabe could see helicopters dropping gracefully onto the concave runway. Next to it was the huge modern Altibar where the ultra-rich gathered to drink and sup with their fortunate friends. Flashes of bright colours flickered down the mountain beside it as skiers manoeuvred on the slopes.

His eyes shifted to the adjoining hotel restaurant. Only a few window tables were occupied yet, all by very elegant diners. Then, he saw his lunch companions. Waiting there for him, to his delight, was not just the French Minister of the Interior, Lionel Jospin, but also the French President, François Marchand.

They were sitting at an isolated table generally reserved for rich patrons or owners of the hotel. Marchand had flown into the *altiport* just minutes earlier in a huge military helicopter. The two Frenchmen were screened off from all other diners yet faced the entrance so that Marchand could survey who was coming into the dining room without being seen himself.

Sitting to their left, at a distance, were two members of the notorious French security service – DGSI. This was the same organisation that, rumour had it, regularly eavesdropped on every telephone conversation in France, and also even in other countries when the President visited them. They also controlled all the resources of the French government, including police commands and overall direction of transportation systems, and energy and electricity supplies for the country. Examples of the organisation's intense loyalty to French political authorities, especially the President, were legion.

As he observed them, Watanabe recalled a well-known scandal that had occurred in July 1985 when French security agents were caught planting bombs to sink the Rainbow Warrior, a Green Peace ship, off the coast of New Zealand. The French inquiry that examined the accusations about government involvement in the affair concluded that the government knew little or nothing about the sabotage.

However, it wasn't long before leaked information contradicted this conclusion and the defence minister resigned. Rather than handing the two saboteurs over to the New Zealand authorities, however, the Paris government incarcerated them in a French Pacific Island prison. Then, after news of the scandal had moved on, authorities delivered them to a prison in France from which they were given an early release and crowned as heroes. It was never admitted that the French President had known every detail about the Rainbow operation. But he actually had ordered it! Regime-sanctioned murder was often rumoured by journalists but they always deferred from putting any details in print.

Watanabe knew that the French interior ministry, which runs domestic security and the police, had dramatically increased its power in recent years – despite criticism that it threatened civil liberties. Emergency laws promulgated by the French government since the steep rise of Islamic terrorism after 2015 now enabled it to order house arrest and use electronic bracelets on anyone it believed was a threat to security or public order. Private property could be searched at any time, places of worship closed, and public gatherings banned. People could even be forced to divulge their passwords for social media – all without judicial oversight. Very useful powers! *The Japanese government could never get away with it*, Watanabe thought.

He approached the table where the French officials awaited him. As a businessman, Watanabe was used to very close relations between businessmen and the leaders of his own party, the Liberal Democratic Party. He greeted the

President of France with a polite but not ingratiating, "Bonjour Monsieur le President. What a great pleasure to see you here. I appreciate your participation in our deal, but I feel even more reassured now that you are actively part of the discussions."

President Marchand did not acknowledge the comment and remained totally impassive. He did not even smile, a common technique designed to unsettle his underlings. Haughty as usual, his behaviour confirmed all the rumours about him. Finally, he curtly addressed Watanabe with, "I'm not here to participate in your dirty little games. I'm here to ensure that the interests of France are protected!" The rest of the world would interpret this outburst as meaning "if *my* interests are protected", but no one would dare say it to his face. Everyone was wary of his rapier-like temper, and of the powerful French security organisation that backed him up with enthusiasm and machine guns – as they did whoever filled the position of top executive.

Administratively, the security service worked directly for Lionel Jospin, the Minister of the Interior, but his career was totally dependent on President Marchand. Both were currently in very tight election situations and needed huge sums of money to overcome their conservative opponents. Sitting next to his boss, looking neat and tidy with his white, carefully trimmed beard, and dapper purple sweater, Lionel Jospin knew exactly what he had to do to stay on good grounds with the President. He had internalised every aspect of the President's identity and concerns.

As Watanabe took his place at the table, Baron de Rothschild appeared, seemingly from nowhere. Probably, Watanabe surmised, he was staying in the hotel, for he

92

emerged in street clothes. De Rothschild was well known at the Annapurna Hotel for being a bisexual who regularly frequented the swimming pool and sauna in search of likeminded, physically fit skiers. The staff joked that he preferred those who could turn a fine slalom into a messy finish. De Rothschild was open and relaxed about his sexual preferences. His one worry was AIDS, a topic he studiously avoided as though he feared even its mention might destroy his lifestyle. He ignored his closest friends who warned that someone you want to have sex with is someone you must be prepared to die for.

De Rothschild's approach was similar to that of Watanabe's but more obvious. He was a sycophant. He fawned on the President. Using flowery, almost philosophical language, he addressed Marchand as if he were a living God. "Monsieur Le President! How grateful we are for your appearance at our little luncheon. I know Chef Michel de Rochedy has prepared a fantastic meal, and he will be by shortly to give his salutations. Ah, here he is now!"

"*Monsieur Le President. Quel honneur!*" the apple-cheeked chef gushed as he approached. "I have prepared a great *repas* for you. Oysters from La Mayenne and Lamb from Tenbeeee in Wales. Would you prefer a little white wine from our area or a petit Puligny-Montrachet from Burgundy to whet your appetite for the meal? And perhaps a fine Bordeaux with the lamb?" With barely a nod of gratitude, the President affirmed he would have the lamb from the queerly named place in Wales, the white wine from Burgundy and the Bordeaux.

The meal began with discussions of everyday life, skiing in Courchevel compared to elsewhere, current issues about families, and the difficult problems Muslim students posed for French schools. As usual, the two politicians huffed and puffed about terrorism without clearly defining the subject. In that way, they could attribute almost any actions or deaths to it so that no significant policy decisions would ever need to be made about it.

The sumptuous meal arrived, and the banal conversation continued. Unsurprisingly, there was no reference to recent scandalous revelations about Marchand's latest mistress or the violence in Courchevel. More surprisingly, neither of Watanabe's companions brought up their impending financial deal. Watanabe knew that both Marchand and Jospin desperately needed money to secure victories in the upcoming elections and he strongly believed that businessmen needed the help of politicians. They needed to work together to merge aspects of four organisations needed for high level corruption – business, government, police and mafia.

Low level or petty crimes in stolen goods and credit card thievery could be carried out without governments and police forces, but sophisticated large-scale criminality involving the transit of funds across state boundaries, like counterfeiting and money laundering, required the collusion of all four organisations to combat modern criminality.

Just before dessert was served, Marchand suddenly rose, said a curt, somewhat imperious goodbye and left the hotel surrounded by his entourage, headed for the *altiport* and on to Paris. As usual, he projected an image of being well above ordinary people. He had to be seen as possessing the legendary virtues of toughness, loyalty, honesty, trustworthiness, duty and sexual probity. He was never to be regarded as someone who simply made deals.

Somewhat shaken by the President's abrupt departure, the three remaining men, Jospin, de Rothschild and Watanabe cut the 'chit chat' and got straight to business. Watanabe spoke first. "I have secured my part of the deal. We can get money from New York and Tokyo. The only new hitch is that we must include the Russians. We need their financial backing. Obviously, Putin and Moscow will not be directly involved. Negotiations will be handled by their agents who are already here in Courchevel. But I can assure you, there is no problem. It is absolutely certain that we will get all the money and assistance needed."

"And," he continued, "don't worry Jospin, ten percent is still confirmed for your party coffers. The question for you, de Rothschild, is simple. Can you keep your part of the bargain? Will the owners sell the properties at our price?"

Behind de Rothschild's polite, dandyish appearance was a very single-minded man driven by one principle – his own interests. "They will," he responded with great assurance, "but they won't sell everything as a package deal. That is final. The owners want to sell their properties individually."

Alarmed, at the prospect of complex and drawn-out negotiations, Watanabe raised his voice well above its usual murmur. "We won't do it. It is not what we agreed. TIM will only deal with the banks after they repossess these properties. They won't deal with the hoteliers one at a time. It's too risky. It's either all the hotels and shops in the region at once or nothing at all."

Jospin, who always spoke in a manner that suggested a minimum of effort with the maximum of sincerity, countered in a conciliatory voice, "We have to settle this now or there will be no deal and we will lose all the work we have done. We are so close."

Watanabe kept his gaze on de Rothschild and, without hesitation, fired back, "You heard me, it must be a quick deal. Either confirm this or let someone take over who can!"

"Look, you fool," Jospin hissed. "We can't just settle it among ourselves. The President has an interest, we have an interest, the owners have an interest, and so do the banks. As you have pointed out, we need the government on our side to proceed, as well as the cash assured from you – yes, and the Russian mafia too. Everyone has to be consulted each time we change a comma in the deal."

Watanabe blanched. He was too controlled to verbally express his shock and shame. He had no intention of admitting that his Russian partners were mafia crooks. Clearly, his TIM Corporation had both legitimate and illegal aspects and their plan required driving down the prices and then buying up large parts of the French Savoie. But he personally could not accept that he would be laundering money for the Russian mafia who clearly were in cahoots with the French. He preferred to think he was dealing with officials of President Putin's government. As an experienced Japanese operator, of course he was aware that important businessmen, like politicians, do have to temper their enthusiasm for honesty when they make big deals. But to risk the press getting wind of dragged-out sales and/or openly admitting that the Japanese deal depended on the mafia or crooks from Russia – never!

Despite his secularism, education and western culture, Watanabe was a strong advocate of Shinto principles and that meant no deals with stupid or violent people who prey on the weak and gullible. That included ordinary people as well as politicians. But dealing with elites, well that was something else. The Japanese language may have no word for intimacy, but it has plenty for snow and being snowed!

"Well, I see," he said crisply. "I'll be in touch." He excused himself and made his way to the toilet. Away from his fellow conspirators, he looked in the mirror, pulled himself up as tall as possible for a man of five-foot-two and decided to act despite these imperious racists and discuss the affair directly with the Russians.

Chapter 7
Russian Mafia
Hotel Byblos De Neige

By the time he left the Annapurna, a chastened Watanabe had arranged to meet his Russian mafia contacts at the Byblos des Neige, a five-star hotel in the Jardin Alpin at the intersection of several ski runs above the village. When he arrived early that evening, the doorman greeted him with a keen eye and a gruff hello. Watanabe boldly returned the man's rude stare. To a large extent, the doorman reflected the change and growing insecurity that the Savoie's top hotels were going through as their financial problems worsened and their prospects dimmed. He was a large, strong looking but ugly man, with one prominent protruding tooth, eyes out of focus, and a generally scruffy demeanour.

The unpleasant doorman leant forward, towering over him. "Can I help you?" he growled. His attitude clearly said, *Your types aren't welcome in this hotel*.

"I'm here to see Yuri. He expects me. He's the leader of the Russian group." Watanabe explained in pidgin English, trying to disguise his distaste for the doorman.

"Okay, I take you, but after you see him, you have to leave the hotel immediately. We take only paying guests here. No casual passers-by or foreign drinkers."

There are about 200 different Russian mafia groups operating globally. They are easily recognisable everywhere by their crude minds, uncouth behaviour and wads of cash. These Russian gangsters, or *mafia,* hang out in the Byblos freely dispensing their money for favours. They do unpalatable things, have no respect for human life, and are highly unpredictable. The tentacles of their criminal enterprises extend throughout Europe, but especially France where authorities say they run a well-structured, quasi-military and sinister organisation. They specialise in influence peddling, extortion and money laundering and are known to have infiltrated the highest echelons of the major European banks to which they deposit money from illegally sold Russian enterprises.

Since around 1990, the word Russian mafia has come to refer to both former communist officials and ordinary criminals. Many fit the stereotype of rugged, good-looking, hard-living James Bond types who carried several passports and could be trusted by their bosses to do anything they were told either abroad or back in Moscow. Some of them are former members of the KGB or the FSB (the new Russian Federal Security Service), other operatives are misfit adventurers. Many are nothing more than sadistic killers.

Some of the mafia work directly for billionaire cronies of President Putin. Their ambition and treachery make them the perfect accomplices to high-level white-collar crime. It is alleged that they carried out the nerve-gas attacks on former Russian spies in London and did other undercover work for the Kremlin. They have a reputation for being violent and erratic. Their dealings in cocaine and prostitution makes them ruthless.

Whatever their backgrounds, these mobsters are widely feared around the world for their proclivity for savagery. They left Russia with its cruelties, injustices and violence and brought their habits to the rest of Europe. Since the early 2000s, it has been widely rumoured that some of the most depraved among them in France had once made eunuchs of their worst enemies, cutting off their penises and gonads, and then rubbing chillies in their wounds to kill the germs before releasing the men back to their families. Other victims had been left barely alive but with ruined bodies and sometimes dangling intestines.

Sitting at a table in the distance Watanabe could see Yuri, his two rough and highly overpaid henchmen with their thick necks and gold chains, along with five family members, including his wife and four children. The wife was preoccupied taking 'selfies' in various poses. The children were engaged in a mock food fight. Watanabe knew that the unpleasant-looking men seated next to their boss Yuri were serial killers. They were also avid skiers. Both had been trained in the well-known Veduchi resort in Russia. He had met them before and, at the time, had thought they exuded an aura of malevolence and death. They both were smoking suggestive-looking cigars. Yuri had a pallid face, a haunted expression, a narrow mouth with a wicked smile, and a near-sighted appearance with his small thick glasses.

As Watanabe approached, he could make out part of their conversation. The boss, Yuri, was wearing a new Loro Piana $35000 jacket he had purchased at Harrods in London. It was considered the most expensive non-fur coat in the world because it had a radiation pocket for cell phones and lots of room for hiding handguns. Evidently, he had already had a lot to drink. Appearing unhinged, he was lording his superior position over the others and making what he considered witty but crude observations about them. Watanabe knew that Yuri provided his bodyguards lavish treatment including expensive ski lessons, but he also loved showing-off and teasing them.

"Of course, we are not a democracy," he was saying. "Do you know the communist book *Animal Farm*? In that novel, everyone believes that all animals are equal. Even the great comrade Napoleon said he would be happy to let people make decisions for themselves. But, you know, they might make the wrong decisions, comrades, and then where would the animals be?"

He paused for effect and then said, "That means you," as he laughed and pointed at Dimitri and Yakof. "We live in a savage world. Or is it a world of savages? Ha-ha."

Then, he abruptly changed topics and began teasing the two henchmen about their wives back in Moscow. "Your women don't even need you anymore," he mocked. "Did you know there is a new thrill pill that allows women to have an instant organism without sex? It is true. A vasoactive peptide drug delivers sexual satisfaction directly to their brains." Seeing the look of disbelief on their stunned faces, he illustrated with his hands. "There is a nerve which leads directly from the cervix to the brain and even a paraplegic who can't feel anything below her waist can have an organism." He roared with laughter. "This makes us no different than animals – the communists and even George Orwell missed that one."

Noticing his Japanese friend watching and slowly approaching, Yuri called out, "Hey, Wat, would you like some wine? I've just ordered another 1997 Mercurey. Costs me 500 Euros, but who cares."

Watanabe drew a chair up to the table and said, "I would adore some wine, thank you. I'm here to discuss business. Perhaps we could have some time in private."

"No. We can do it right here. We are with family," Yuri responded drunkenly. "Get on with it. What's the problem?"

Embarrassed to have to speak in front of two glaring henchmen, an extremely damaged and tarted-up wife, and young children, Watanabe took a deep breath, glanced around, and mumbled softly, "We need your two billion dollars but you and the French security service are going much too far. You have been causing accidents – even killing people? Why? We don't need this. It's going to get us in big trouble."

Gulping down a full glass of the vintage wine, Yuri released another of his tirades. He always tried to impress lesser associates, especially when he was drunk.

"The French security system is none of your business, slant eyes. And neither are our methods. They work for us and we work for them. We are a team. As long as we do our jobs, get the prey, and share the profits nobody tells us what to do. Certainly not you Japs."

Watanabe did not respond to this boorish insult. Something else was bothering him. "I think I saw the Muslims twins in the village – the same ones you hired in Paris to bomb Notre Dame. Are they here working for you?" He barely got it out.

"We brought them. And we bought them. Sometimes it works, sometimes it doesn't," Yuri acknowledged. "Our government is against Islamic extremists and ISIL, but that does not prevent us from using them in our work. They can be useful. Did you know there was a near explosion on the Mall in London last week? Neat operation. Nearly worked. One of our Muslim friends took room 306 in a Gentlemen's Club on Pall Mall so he could shoot a bazooka at the Queen during the trooping of the colours. Too bad it turned out to be a stand-in. How were they to know the Queen would be home with a cold?

"We'll try again. It was fantastic. Our handsome, Syrian, Oxford-educated Muslim just paid his bill, walked out of the Club carrying his bag, and no one was any the wiser. That's the kind of precision these guys bring to an operation and it's why we use them. They have contacts, are ruthless, and can be trusted – as long as they are well paid."

Watanabe looked incredulous. "How exactly could your Muslim get into a prestigious London Club? Why weren't they stopped by the doormen or the security staff?"

"They follow a simple formula." Yuri replied with a grin. "When they are with the Club's staff, they act like they are members. And when they are with the members, they act like they are staff. It works every time!"

Yuri took a swig of wine, then went on to brag in detail about how the mafia and their Muslim jihadist friends were cooperating to bring the hotel owners of the Savoie region to their knees. "To prepare the ground, a few people have had to die over the last few months. When possible, we make their deaths look like ski accidents. The woman in the yellow car was different. That murder was not planned by us. It was stupidly done at the last minute by the twin female jihadists. But it was good for us anyway. They are careful. You know it wasn't their fault that the gas canisters at Notre Dame did not explode a few weeks ago. ISIS has trained these women well. They are most useful, handy with knives and revolvers, very good at close-range. But maybe undertrained in explosives. They are also easily dispensable if something goes wrong."

Yuri was on a roll. He liked nothing better than an audience to admire his exploits. "Young women around the world are lured to the Middle East to marry Islamic fighters and bear them children. Now that ISIS is losing in Iraq and Syria, they train their females to be suicide bombers and killers elsewhere. Many of them are in Europe now looking for work. We hired the twins and brought them here. They are good. With the help of the French security service, they killed that Brit Worthington. He is too nosy. They will shoot the bastard in cold blood. No compassion. No traces."

Watanabe felt sick. Down deep, he was a moral man, and this behaviour, he thought, epitomised the banal attitude toward murder that he often detected in the Russian mafia and jihadists. He also knew what Yuri neglected to say. Sophisticated operations took brains and were carried out by the Russians themselves. The earlier crippling and destruction of the giant ski lift with its multiple deaths could have been their work. They must have coordinated the preparation and inserted the fatal flawed chip in the computer well before the ski season began.

As if he could read Watanabe's mind, Yuri gloated, "It was fantastic when the *téléphérique* fell off. It was supposed to fall off, you know." He paused to empty the bottle in his glass.

"Another Mercurey!" he yelled to the waiter.

"The French security service is pretty good too," Yuri continued with satisfaction. "Wherever our guys go in France, they bug the place for us. That's how we found out about that nosey Brit, Worthington. The security service listened to his call to someone over in another ski station. They gave me a recording of him telling what he had overheard you guys talking about at the Chabichou Bar. So, our boys sent the two young female Muslims to shut him up."

The children at the table were getting bored and restless. One had knocked over her drink. "Go on" – Yuri waved – "go swim, ski, whatever you want." They didn't hesitate. Nor did their mother. They got up from the table in haste and headed to another room.

As the new bottle of Mercurey was being poured into fresh glasses, he continued, "The French can tap into telephone calls and computer messages whenever they want. They keep in close touch. If anyone else gets wind of our plot we will kill them too. These murders don't hurt us. They are getting some press now, and that is good. The publicity scares people and lowers the price our friends will have to pay for the properties. We don't need to worry about the police. The Prosecutor for Paris is in charge of all terrorist investigations in France. He has little time for our little regional challenge here in the Savoie. Besides he's in the pocket of the French President and the Minister of Security."

Watanabe exploded. "But who is the guy the Brit spoke with? Who else did he talk to at the hotel?"

"We've got that covered too. The American will die tomorrow."

Watanabe threw up his hands in exasperation. This was a culture and a way of speaking he wanted nothing to do with. He was a cunning and tactical man but not a killer. "I suppose there is no virtue like necessity," he mumbled as he suddenly rose, turned, and left to think about the mafia and jihadis and how he could disassociate himself from them.

He was surprised and offended when the security guard demanded to search him as he departed from the hotel. "You think I stole the cutlery? You know a country is in trouble when goons search you on the way *out* of buildings. It is a grave new world." he muttered to himself.

Chapter 8
Jihadi Twin Brides: Club Hotel

They arrived by bus on Saturday in the long convoy of vehicles at the height of the massive snowstorm. It had been a harrowing trip. Cautiously, the two young women emerged from the warm vehicle into the cold air. With great effort, they tugged their suitcases along the snowy sidewalk to their designated hotel at the base of the village. Their sparsely furnished room on the second floor of the small, inexpensive Club Hotel had only one narrow double bed which two people would normally have found unpleasant to sleep in, but this was no ordinary couple. They were inseparable Muslim twins and they were jihadis. Exhausted, they fell on the bed without unpacking and slept for several hours.

The girls awoke simultaneously at dawn on Sunday, rolled out of bed, knelt on their prayer mats, recited their morning prayers, then quickly unpacked their suitcases, and pulled on their new Parisian clothes. It felt strange. They looked like ordinary teenage French girls with their thin bodies in skinny jeans, tight sweaters and medium long black hair.

Ready for the day, Safiya and Tashfeen gazed out the small, frosted window of their hotel room. It was small and dirty but they could still see the resort area was awesome. The sky had turned a light grey with a slight haze and, in the background, they could see a daytime moon resting on the vapours of a modern jet aircraft above the mountains. It was a beautiful almost-surreal image. The dagger-like image in the sky reminded them of their black and white Caliphate flag. But the room was nothing like the small, bare, windowless apartment they had called home in Syria.

Safiya sighed and was the first to speak. "It is glorious, but we can't hang about. We need to meet the Russians this afternoon at the Aparthotel, but before then we have a lot to do." Tashfeen looked wistful. "They say they will pay a lot a money. Maybe it will be enough to bring our families to Europe so we can begin a new life. *Inshallah*."

This forlorn hope was all that remained after their hurried escape from Syria. The romanticism that had led them to the Middle East in the first place was long gone. Europe was not home, but perhaps a new life could happen here.

The twins' long, convoluted route to Courchevel had been highly unusual. Born to a lower class, immigrant Iraqi Muslim family in St Paul, Minnesota, a large centre of Muslim culture in the United States, the pair had lived a relatively normal early childhood in the suburbs. They attended regular primary and high schools in the Twin Cities, and in their early years were so bound by family and each other that they gave little thought to how different they were from other students. But they were unique.

Their family was devoted to the religious and social teachings of the prophet Mohammed. From a young age they prayed five times a day on prayer mats, obediently covered their heads with scarves, and did their parents bidding. They rarely mixed with Western children. Their social life was limited to family and the mosque, and once a week they ate out at a small halal restaurant where their parents went as much to meet other Muslims as for the food.

To a large extent, the twins were the hapless victims of poverty and their religion, and as they grew older and became more aware of the society around them, they developed a confused mix of emotions and concerns about their identity. At school, their teachers told them how lucky they were to be Americans because they were free to become whatever they wanted. They just needed to work hard and "lean in" and they could become rich and share the American dream.

By high school, many of their peers were openly sexually active, cared mostly about movie and pop stars, and took great pains to learn about and imitate them. They didn't seem to care much about their own parents or believe in God. Like many other young Muslim girls, instead of fitting in, the twins became self-conscious, inward looking, passive, and self-doubting. They learnt to think they were controlled by God and fate. At school, they were eager to please others, passive and obedient to those who could help them lead a life devoted to their values of God, marriage, and children.

They also thought of themselves as among the least worthy Americans, nourished by familiar family stories about persecution, and failure in the United States. Personal humiliations, taunts and slights, both minor and major, created doubts that they would ever achieve a happy and prosperous future. They concluded that their teenage peers were largely envious and ignoble. But, unlike many of their male Muslim counterparts, the twins did not develop political attitudes or join others to try to redress the social evils that they thought conflicted with Allah and the teachings of the Koran.

Neither of the twins felt particularly pretty or desirable; they became aware that very few boys their age were interested in them. As dispirited young teens with unmet emotional needs, they took refuge on the Internet for companionship. Their family worked in the city most of the day, so when the two came home from school, they had many hours of liberty to participate in social media on their iPads and computers. The Internet brought novel ways to communicate and compare their lives to those of other girls. They learnt how teenagers hook up, break up, and take drugs, but, unlike many adolescents, they soon got bored with what they sneeringly agreed was drivel, mere "chick lit" and "prick lit", and began to search for more serious material on the Web.

By late high school, a few of the Muslim boys they knew of had already begun to rebel against their families and lead independent lives, some even as petty criminals. The girls were aware that many local boys of all religions and social classes were involved in illicit activities of one kind or another in their late teens, though they usually stopped by their late 20s. The twins were determined not follow these routes. They were impressionable and each in her own way became fascinated with internet messages about America's "evil activities" in Muslim lands. They found exciting videos online about life as a jihadi. They joined chat groups with other Muslim girls. They also found inspiring videos by Islamist preachers, with extremist content, and romantic tales of Muslim heroism in the Middle East.

When Donald Trump was running to be President of the United States, they were terrified by things he said about

Muslims. They were confused and angered by constant hints and suggestions that their religion was subversive and evil. They began to reject what they saw as Western, and particularly Christian views of their beliefs, and to imagine their own ideal world and life within a future Islam. Slowly, they embraced Islamist views of victimisation, jihad, and Sharia law, and looked for information about the worldwide Caliphate as organised by the Islamic State of Iraq and Syria.

They were excited by "dawah", the practice of preaching the message of Islam to non-Muslims. Mohammed had envisaged Islam as the one true religion and ultimate mission of all prophets, and had asked non-Muslims to join his cause. The twins dreamt of an Islamic utopia. Their objection to nihilism, or lack of significant meaning in life, led them to consider what it would mean to fight and die for a just cause. *Perhaps*, they thought, *only extreme behaviour such as jihadi suicidal action could win them a place in an Islamic nirvana.*

It is evident that all religious sects try to keep their holy texts watertight from criticism. And secular people in the West have great difficulty understanding those individuals who are religious devotees, especially those who combine it with grudges against the American culture and politics. But to understand jihadis, it is imperative to understand the interaction of these beliefs.

Because of the complexity and ambiguity of human experience, human nature has both fixed and non-fixed constructs. Some traits remain constant throughout all cultures and religions. Young people everywhere ask essential questions about life and death. If questions such as, Who am I? Who are you? Who are they? are not answered by families or schools, other socialisation institutions fill the vacuum – churches, mosques, universities, governments, prisons, mass communications, and especially the Internet. The dissemination of radical ideas by these means crosses boundaries of nation, ideology, class and even gender. The global Internet is an ideal instrument both for feeding anger and creating submissive feelings. Action based on these emotions has a moral simplicity easily adopted to modern times and psychology.

According to Islamist philosophy, the Western model fails women in particular. The twins totally agreed. Like many other young Muslims in the west, they were isolated and progressively excluded from their societies. They felt they had only limited prospects. They were vulnerable and particularly hurt when their identity and appearance became social and political battlegrounds. It bothered them that their religion was portrayed as incompatible with western, and especially American, values.

When you arrive in Syria, you will not have to act like western women. You will not be obliged to wear their clothes, they read online. *Modesty dress is recognised, head scarfs and other religious symbols are welcomed and encouraged.*

Safiya and Tashfeen were particularly incensed when they heard that the French outlawed even the burkini bathing suit that allows Muslim women to swim in modesty.

"We do our best to comply with their values and they still attack us. Even when we dress with care and don't bother anyone, it is not acceptable," Tashfeen often complained.

Online, the girls found that ISIS recruiters promised to protect girls and welcome them to their community. They were lured by offers of empowerment, purpose and the romantic element of joining a godly cause. "A utopia awaits

112

you in Syria where your piety and courage will make you genuine heroines of Islam." The twins loved the positive approach and were encouraged by estimates that of the girls who adhere to the Islamic State of Iraq and Syria (ISIS) about one out of every five recruits came from Europe. If they went to the Middle East, they would not be alone.

The ISIS internet radicalisation programme introduced the twins to other girls their age who were intoxicated with radical Islamist ideas. Then, after they were emotionally engaged with their new online community, and as they advanced in the bloom of their lives, the girls were lined up with boys of a similar age who had already gone to Iraq to fight for the Caliphate. Safiya and Tashfeen felt empowered by the attention to their interests and values and became total converts. They became, as they each described it, "a whole human being".

After months of priming on the net, each fell wildly in love with a European Islamic fighter. The boys, one from Marseilles France and the other from Malenbeek Belgium, were a couple years older than the twins and had been radicalised by clerics in their local town mosques. They had joined ISIS, been trained, and fought from village to village with them in Iraq. Eventually they were moved to the capital of Raqqa, Syria about 100 miles from the former Iraq border. The fighters convinced their new girlfriends to join them there.

The parents of the twins were terrified and did their best to prevent their daughters from leaving. They listed a morass of dangerous problems in the Middle East and promised the girls that if they stayed home, they could have more freedom. There was no need for them to go off to a foreign country.

"You are deserting your family", "You'll never feel at home anywhere", "You will never find a good husband over there", "You will die and become jihadi widows".

But it was too late.

Pro-Caliphate adherents in Minnesota helped the twins travel incognito to Paris and on to Turkey, where they were issued fake passports, and taken across the border into Syria. Once there, the twins joined many other young recruits, seventeen percent of whom were female and many in their early twenties. Within a short time, they discovered a new sense of community and authority and incorporated all aspects of Islam into their lives.

The twins attended Koran classes, learnt Arabic pronunciation, and Islamic practices, and graduated from covering their hair and faces to wearing burqas, full body clothing that hid their slight figures. They dressed completely in black, even their underclothes; colour was *haram* or forbidden. They listened to female religious leaders, learnt Sharia law, came to openly despise infidels, and began using banks offering Sharia services.

Their teachers outlined what they considered the moral vacuity of a dying liberal world, but did not tell the girls how much their modern jihadi discourse hid aspects of radical western thought about the utility of violence and revolution. Instead, they were taught martial arts, how to handle guns and knives, wear suicide belts, and master the basics of making primitive bombs, including how to mix products from local beauty-supply outlets for making explosive detonators. *We are so lucky*, the girls thought. In earlier years, women were not normally allowed to fight as they had other important support roles in conflict. But now, with ISIS losing territory, it needed more helping hands.

The girls accepted the jihadi view that accomplishing goals for the Caliphate required taking innocent lives. The victims would be mere collateral damage on the path towards righteousness. They fought for Allah to halt the continued moral decline and corruption of infidels.

The twins took up all the familiar jihadi mantras: "Allah Akbar", "God is great", "Defend Muslims", "Allah gave us emancipation", "Allah gave us beauty", and "We are Muslims and we don't fear death".

Not only did they admire and love the two European boys they had joined with, they embraced the ideas of sexuality and marriage found in the Koran. They learnt that homosexuality was for beasts, not humans, and that anal sex was unacceptable. They were taught that the death sentence is an appropriate punishment for gays. They memorised the results of a recent Gallop poll which found that zero percent of Muslims thought homosexual acts were morally acceptable.

The girls knew that they would be socially ostracised from their new family and friends in Syria if they did not adhere strictly to the principles of Islam. They wanted to fit in, to belong. They went through a *nikkah*, or wedding ceremony, devoted themselves to their husbands, and supported them in their causes. They quickly became pregnant. After each gave birth to a boy, they raised them to the age of two, and then happily released them to a religious school that would teach them devotion to the art of jihad and instil in them the Caliphate's religion of world hatred.

During the girls' years in the Middle East, however, the ISIS bid to project influence and power there was failing, and their territory began to shrink. They were losing several major armed battles in northern Iraq and Syria and many Islamists had begun to move to other countries to fight on new fronts. Two favourite places for Islamic refugees were Libya and Afghanistan. Some fighters headed for various places in west and central Africa while a few even made their way to far off areas such as the Mindanao in the Philippines. Many others headed back to their homelands in America and Europe to continue their work there.

After Mosul fell, Iraqi troops, anti-regime Sunnis, Turkish Kurds, and American forces tightened their grip around Raqqa. Many ISIS fighters died, leaving their young wives with a bleak future. Bombing was frequent. Many buildings were destroyed and cities lacked running water, electricity and food supplies much of the time. Schools and hospitals were hit. Even primitive medical care was no longer available. The twins' husbands encouraged their American wives to leave their children behind, depart for Europe, and fight for the cause there. They agreed to meet them in France as soon as they could.

The women fled disguised as refugees, making their way through Turkey into Eastern Europe. It took one harrowing month to arrive in a French Calais camp as part of a Middle East refugee group. From there the girls were thrilled to be moved to Paris. They initially lived in a small tent community near the metro Stalingrad in the heart of the city where they met enterprising refugees and criminals. The camp was a wretched smelly stink hole with no sanitary facilities or water. There was no alternative but to use the sidewalks and streets for their needs, and the refugees were hassled daily by the police.

The meagre finances the girls brought with them quickly ran out. Without passports, visas, or *carnets* to allow them to work legitimately in France, they were destitute. Prostitution was out of question, being against their Muslim principles, new and old. Instead, they sought employment with petty criminal and terrorist organisations where their background and qualifications carried some weight. It wasn't long before they met members of the Russian mafia, who gave them small jobs to test their abilities.

Successful terrorist attacks in European capital cities in the recent past had already frayed nerves all over the continent. The worst of them, which occurred just before the girls got to Paris, was the famous 2015 attack on the Bataclan Night club when the rock group *Eagles of Death* played. Ninety people were slaughtered and left blood over a centimetre deep. It looked like an "abattoir", they were told.

Among the twins' first assignments, they were instructed to make and conceal a bomb in a small Citroen near Notre Dame Cathedral. The device was discovered by the police before it could detonate, but even news of the attempt served a purpose, frightening more tourists away from the major attractions at the centre of the City of Lights. The mafia and their terrorist allies deliberately attempted to provoke state overreaction, and when the authorities regularly fell for their ploys, they created even more problems for democratic leaders.

While the twins were in hiding after the failed Notre Dame event, their Russian mafia contact, a man called Yuri, sent them to Courchevel in the French Alps for new and more important tasks. The girls were glad to leave their refugee camp and delighted by the trip through the French countryside and the mountains. The pastoral views in the early part of the trip reminded them of their first home.

On their difficult bus ride up the mountain, they could not help but wonder what it must be like to live in a ski village compared with Minnesota or Syria. In the Alps, there seemed to be very few people or houses and the mountainous region looked peaceful, almost haunted. Even in the storm, the young women were dazzled by the twinkling, subdued lights in the otherwise dark villages, and marvelled at the beauty around them. They remembered Minnesota as always being grey, white and black in the winter. Syria was brown and dusty all year long with thousands of desperate people and ruins everywhere. But they had their faith to support them.

When they arrived at their hotel in the village of Courchevel 1850, the young women's first job was to let the Russians know that they were there. They were aware of the brutal reputation that clung to their employers and knew to be very careful. The Russians instructed them to appear the next afternoon at a location in the middle of the town, and warned that in the meantime they were not to speak to anyone about why they were there in the village.

Early that morning, however, they saw no harm in phoning their husbands in Raqqa to tell them they had arrived. They spoke openly and excitedly, describing their trip, and their new Russian mafia bosses, guessing what they might be asked to do, and assessing how much they might be paid.

As the initial excitement of the call wore off, they heard a noise in the hall outside their room. Tashfeen quickly opened the door to discover a cleaning lady eavesdropping on their conversation. The twins knew they were in deep trouble. The woman almost certainly had learnt something about their background, refugee status, connection to Syria, and perhaps even their upcoming meeting. They knew that Yuri would be furious if he ever found out about the telephone call.

Instinctively, in unison, they yanked the woman into the room. While Tashfeen upbraided the woman for eavesdropping, Sofiya bashed her head with a water bottle. The woman crumpled. They knew what they had to do. It was something they had prepared for in Raqqa, a clear end-means calculation. If the woman disclosed anything she had overheard, they might never see their husbands or children again. Killing her would be a morally justified homicide.

Tashfeen saw the woman's handbag on the trolley, and rifled through it until she found the car keys. Taking a clean sheet from the top of the stack of bedding on the trolley, she draped it over the woman's shoulders. Between them, the twins hoisted the dazed woman to her feet and hauled her down the hallway to the exit. "We are taking you to your car" Tashfeen said gently. "Is it in the lot?" The woman nodded and mumbled "the yellow one." The young women half dragged her out the exit and through the deep snow to the edge of the hotel parking lot behind the cinema. The car was easy to spot, parked somewhat precariously at the edge of the drop to a ski run.

Safiya opened the door and shoved the woman into the small yellow Volkswagen. Shaking with fear and cold, they glanced around. No one could see them as they executed the skills that they had learnt as jihadists for the first time. Tashfeen slipped into the car beside the woman then quickly grabbed her by her hair and turned her head quickly to expose the fleshy side nearest her sister Safiya who immediately drew a sharp knife blade along her carotid artery. The shocked

119

woman did not struggle. Blood splattered everywhere, pouring onto the seat and car floor. Safiya threw the bed sheet over the dead woman's head, locked the doors, and the pair hurried back to their hotel.

The twins quickly disposed of their blood splattered clothes and tidied their room. Safiya moved the woman's cart to the other end of the hall. Within minutes they left the hotel to replace their soiled clothes. The arcade was only a short walk away, brightly lit and filled with beautiful displays. They were astonished by the outrageous cost of even simple clothing in Courchevel 1850 and by the vast array of colours and textures in the resort clothing. Overwhelmed, they left for a cheaper outdoor market area they had seen below their hotel. By the time they had made their purchases they needed to eat. "Let's try the Spanish restaurant near our hotel," Sofiya suggested. It was a popular lunch spot and was very busy when the pair arrived. They were forced to share a table with an elderly crippled woman near the back of the room. She looked odd in her bright, red hat, but quite harmless, so the girls sat down.

For a while, they ignored her and settled on their orders.

Finally, the woman spoke in English, "You don't look like regulars, or French, or even skiers. You look," she said staring at both of them, "like Americans." They didn't answer, but politely asked the woman about herself. As the lonely cripple picked at her zucchini, she appeared pleased to talk to someone. It wasn't long before the twins realised just how lonely and physically and psychologically broken the woman was. They were captivated and their discussion with the stranger struck an emotional chord with them. It felt good to talk, and they even offered to buy the woman's lunch as the woman launched into stories of her sad childhood, life in the Aussie outback, her abusive marriage, and then a nervous breakdown.

The woman had been born in a squalid gypsy camp in Romania. As a young teen, she was abused by her father and kicked out of her home by her mother who blamed her for her father's transgressions. With no formal education or training, she made her living as a prostitute travelling around Europe before she bought a special immigrant, one-way, cheap fifty-pound sea trip to Darwin, Australia. There, she met and quickly married a man who lived near the harbour, in a small outback settlement. It wasn't long before she discovered what an abusive scoundrel he was, and couple years later, after much suffering and abuse, she left him.

The story that had the greatest impact on the twins was one that showed what a real bastard the husband was. Once when she was in her house in the village of Nooambah, Northern Territories, her husband's best friend came to visit, introduced himself, and told her he wanted to check out the spare bedroom on the upper floor. The two of them climbed the stairs and entered the bedroom to find two people huddling under the covers. It his wife and her husband. The enraged stranger ripped the covers off the bed, pointed his Glock 17 revolver at the naked lovers, but then thought better of it and ran back down the stairs leaving them startled but alive. She wished he had shot them both!

To the twins, it sounded like something from a bad movie – the worst of life in America. Enthralled, Safiya burst out, "Then what happened?"

There were more violent struggles with her husband and eventually she returned to Europe. By chance, she ended up in Courchevel, France. She had been here for almost twenty years and loved it. She was quite crippled now from various accidents and severe arthritis. She lived on welfare, but she worked when she could, taking photos and doing favours for tourists. Sometimes the local police gave her surveillance jobs too, she said. She loved life here but was worried about new outside influences she was seeing in the village. She thought serious problems might be coming. She looked thoughtfully at the girls but didn't elaborate. "I don't like change," she said.

The twins were mesmerised but knew they had work to do. They paid the bill, and thanked the woman before heading back to their hotel. They were happy to have met her but were left very depressed and emotional. They were often torn between kindness and duty as well as between Western and Muslim values. They were aware that their behaviour had also fluctuated wildly in Courchevel and not only because they were dizzy with the high altitude.

Back at the hotel, the young women quickly dressed in their new winter clothes and headed out to meet their mafia contacts. A few steps from the entrance there was a very young boy lying on the sidewalk crying and screaming in pain. No one was around, so the twins instinctively bent down to help him. They soon discovered the actual problem. When he had tried to do up the zipper of his ski pants after going to the toilet, he had caught the skin of his testicle in the zip. The twins deftly jerked the zipper to release his skin. He redoubled his screaming but they knew that in a few seconds, he would be all right.

Passers-by, attracted by the child's screams, began to crowd around, and before the girls could leave, the child's terrified parents came running from a nearby shop. They embraced their sobbing child and reflexively began to berate the two girls for molesting him. "Bloody perverts!" the man yelled. "I'm going to report you to the police!" The girls turned and ran, hoping no one would follow them.

The hatred and anger directed against them on this occasion left the sisters very angry. They had only been trying to help, but cultural differences, their foreign accent and ignorance of the intricacies of the French language made them easy targets of blame. As they hustled down the snowy sidewalk, Safiya asked softly, "Why can't people accept kindness from strangers? We were only trying to help."

"I don't know," Tashfeen replied, "but do you remember the Italian mafia leader in the movie *Godfather*? The one who helped people and was generous, but could still kill when he needed to? I think we are like him, only we kill for Allah."

"True," Tashfeen replied bitterly. "But, how did we get into this mess Safiya? When do we get to live our own lives? We always have to follow orders. Now we have to do whatever the Emir and these Russians order us to do. Will it never end?"

Perhaps the philosopher Santayana had situations like this in mind when he said that fanatics are people who redouble their efforts when they have lost their purpose. As children, the twins had never hurt anyone or even told a lie, but now in adulthood they did both. They were clearly conflicted. They had fond memories of their parents, home, husbands, and children, and natural warm responses to those who needed help. Yet, as true believers they accepted and were prepared to die for their new ideology, even as suicide terrorists. They worried that they had only shabby futures in store.

In a few minutes, the girls approached two large, glowering Russians in the coffee shop in the Aparthotel. They were cautious. Clearly, their visceral suspicion was mutual. The Russian greetings were sharp and cold. "Have you talked to anyone? Has anyone followed you?"

"No one knows we are here and no one has followed us. We had a problem with a nosey house cleaner, but we took care of it." The detailed story of the Portuguese housekeeper enraged the Russians. The twins did not bother to mention their conversation with the 'zucchini' woman or the attention they had drawn trying to help a little boy in distress.

"That was stupid! Really stupid," the first Russian, Dimitri, growled before Yakof interjected, "Did you remove all evidence? Did anyone see you?"

"It's okay. No, there is no problem. We knew what we were doing. No one saw us. We left no fingerprints or clues whatsoever. The snow covered everything outside the car. There is only *her* blood on the clothes and in the car."

Examining them intently, the Russian finally spoke. "Well then, we may have some simple tasks for you. Come to the Cat's bar at the Chabichou hotel near here tonight at 8 pm for further instructions. Don't be conspicuous and don't talk to anyone. No more communication with your husbands or anyone else by phone or Internet. No phone calls, period!"

The girls felt queasy, but nodded in agreement. They knew they were dispensable. They knew these goons would rather flay or even flense them than let them go if they did anything to harm their cause.

Chapter 9
Unravelling the Plot
Hotel Les Airelles

The snowstorm had finally petered out and light clouds and decent weather were on the horizon, but no one in the advanced ski class felt much like skiing. Peter's death weighed heavily on everyone. Those who had most admired the Brit's sunny, plucky personality went through the motions of lining up to explore the mountain and its secret skiing delights, but they were too distracted. It was no fun. It provided no escape. Conversations kept returning to the homicide. Jim and Robert were so depressed with the emotional chatter that they left the class early and headed up to the famous and beautiful hotel Les Airelles for a drink. They were anxious to talk privately.

The hotel was Robert's favourite. He knew a lot about its background, history, and qualities. For many years, the grand building had been the venue for upscale academic conferences. Particularly in the 1950s, 1960s and 1970s, Americans, Canadians, and the British had often held their academic retreats at Les Airelles, a reflection of the fact that the meetings were lavishly sponsored by NATO and its sister foundations with the stated goal of maintaining a united defence strategy against the USSR during the Cold War.

In those days, after a day's work and the consumption of much fine or not-so-fine wine, professors' discussions would turn from criticising the ideology of the USSR and debating each country's proper share of the NATO defence budget to arguments and gossip about colleagues, women, and cultural issues.

Today, of course, the situation is reversed. Funding agencies are far less generous and the formal agendas of international relations conferences are now dominated by politically correct talks on identity, gender, race studies, women, family, sex, clothing, fashions and the like. Participants only tepidly take on the broader and perhaps more controversial topics of macro/microeconomics, trade policy, terrorism, or even the foreign policy actions of Russia in Eastern Europe and the Middle East. In the era of me-academics, disagreements derive more from academic posturing, the search for status, and the narcissism of minor cultural and ethnic differences. People seem more anxious to get revenge for grievances than to protect their countries. *Taking 'selfies'*, Robert thought, *characterises the change of focus as well as anything.*

When funding for academic conferences was slashed in the 1980s, there were dramatically fewer American, Canadian, and British conferences in elite places like Les Airelles, so these hotels shifted their sights to a richer clientele, pricing academics out of their markets. The top hotels became very posh and began attracting more and more elite clients from the oil rich states of the Middle East and even Russia.

Today, if there were any place one could relax in style in Courchevel, this would be it. Clients do not go there for fake gold objects or kitsch. The luxurious Airelles – or properly Hotel Charme les Airelles – is a massive, exquisite mountain chalet, fashioned from red cedar and white stone. Inside, the entrance floor come from an ancient castle, the walls are decorated with beautiful paintings and small deer heads that were trophies from former hunting parties. The thickly carpeted lounge and bar areas resemble those of a Venetian villa, and feature two gigantic open fireplaces. The atmosphere is serene and sophisticated.

It is the a for the rich and fabulous, attracting oligarchs, members of the jet set, their kids, bodyguards and mistresses. Familiar guests include such luminaries as the Spanish royals, David Beckham, and Prince William and his family. Fittingly, the hotel requires gentlemen to wear jackets and ladies elegant attire after ski hours. Each outfit would cost more than a worker's monthly salary.

The pair of distraught skiers took in the scene with pleasure, then headed directly to the bar. Robert, who would much rather have been staying here than in a pension mile away in the less classy resort of Méribel, felt another pang of annoyance that he had booked so late. Jim, as a subsidised government highflyer, would never consider the possibility. He would be refunded for his stay at the basic Courcheneige hotel. It was nowhere near the standard of Les Airelles, but he was grateful to be lodged there and not in the inexpensive Club Hotel at the bottom of the village, or even in a lower village, like many other Canadian public servants. By the awed look on his face, one could easily guess this was his first visit to Les Airelles.

As they entered the bar, Jim's cell phone vibrated. He excused himself to take the call privately. He expected it would be his wife who would be back in Calgary by now, but it wasn't. He was surprised to hear a familiar voice from his head government office in Ottawa, Canada.

"Jim, how's it going? How is your French coming along?" he heard one of his bosses asking. "I hope you have made a lot of progress." Without waiting for a reply, he said "We're going to need you home sometime soon."

"Everything is fine, Jack. What's up?"

"Not much, I just wanted to warn you that you will be getting a call from some officials at the CSIS (Canadian Security Intelligence Service). Apparently, they have some new intel and perhaps some task for you over there in Europe."

"Christ, what's that all about?"

"They aren't telling me. I don't have a clue. But they gave me the contact's number and name. He is Larry Wilcox, CSIS Associate Director for emergency planning, and his cell number is 613-3358819. He is going to get in touch with you soon. If you don't hear from him within a day or so, you may want to ring him."

"But why? I have no relationship to CSIS and don't want one! What's it about?"

"How the hell am I supposed to know, Jim? This is a Conservative government after all. Just giving you a heads up." Having said that, he hung up.

Jim slowly worked his way back to Robert, who had already ordered them each a lager and some crisps. Robert laughed. "What's up? Is your wife wanting you to check up on the kids or to pick up the laundry?" he teased.

Peter had told him Jim's story. The Canadian was in France on language training for the better part of the year. He had begun the school term in Paris with his family, however, his industrious wife kept returning home to Calgary to assist in her university law department and work part-time for the New Democratic party. She had come with the family to the Courcheneige, but quickly left saying she would visit them in Paris whenever she could. Peter had interpreted this to mean rarely, as she had said she vastly preferred toiling with political colleagues to wasting time on 'wifely or mothering functions.' Besides, Peter had said, her French was lousy.

Robert had gathered that Jim was a devoted father, constantly busy with his pre-teen boys. He didn't resent his wife's absence, and was openly delighted to be with them, and escape the bitter weather and routine life in Calgary. Representing the federal government in discussions of provincial power and security in international affairs could get quite boring in Calgary. Now, the boys were enrolled in local Parisian schools but Jim still spent most of his free time bringing them up to speed in math and language so they would fit back into their school when they returned home.

Jim smiled but didn't take the bait. "Nothing like that. Just a routine call from Ottawa. So, tell me Robert, what's your theory about Peter's murder?" His scepticism was obvious.

Robert quickly filled his friend in on everything he knew about the background and real estate scheme as told to him by Peter. "Of course, it is all conjecture," he concluded glumly. "Peter's claim that he heard the conversation in a bar while he was drinking is no proof of anything." Jim agreed. He was not impressed. Indeed, he was suspicious of all 'third-hand' talk, as he called it. *Drunken* third-hand talk was in a stupid category all of its own.

The two men ordered more lagers. "What do you really know about Peter?" Robert asked. Jim confessed he had barely met him and so couldn't say much. He had talked more with Sue, and found her very charming. He found the bare outline of Peter's story bizarre. Clearly, Peter had been murdered after he told Robert what he learnt about a plot to gain ownership of the major hotels and property in the Savoie, but Jim was dubious of any causal connection. Rather than be negative though, he asked how he could help.

Robert was silent for a few moments, then he responded slowly, "There is no point in going to the police yet. First, we need to be absolutely certain that there is a criminal conspiracy and who is in on it. If it is true, and conspirators did kill Peter, then I can find a way to stop them. I can broadcast it to the world on CNN. I still have a few contacts there. Exposing the perpetrators to the world would blow the lid off the whole thing. But I need to be sure! How can we get proof? Has anything suspicious happened in the Courcheneige hotel? Does Sue know anything?"

"Not that I know of," Jim responded. "I doubt Peter would have said anything to her. He was very protective of her and she seemed genuinely unable to comprehend what happened when Peter was murdered. Somebody was badly hurt in the hotel a few days ago but that was just an accident. It couldn't have been related to Peter's murder. A guy fell in his bathroom – split his head open on the glass doors of the bathtub. I didn't know him. Likely he simply fell down. Anyone who has been in one of those narrow, claustrophobic, steamy bathrooms knows just how easy it would be to slip and hit your head on the glass.

"But everybody knows that there have been a lot of other bad accidents in the area this year," he went on, "way more than in other years. I doubt that they can be related to this so-called plot, but it's worth considering. There were the disastrous cable cars. Then, there was that murdered woman dumped down the mountain in the yellow car. How could that be related?" The only other criminal event that Jim had heard about was this morning's petty case of stolen skis. It was a scandal only because the police decided to go after some young ski thieves rather than following up on Peter's murder or other more serious crimes."

"It's bizarre. Why would the police act like that? Unless of course, they were ordered off the cases by some higher-ups?"

Robert smiled but was intrigued. "French police and security could be involved. Perhaps government leaders are trying to get a rake-off of some sort on a property deal? That would be believable. I've seen it before. They have tight control of security. I wonder if there is any way we could find out more about the security aspects of this operation?"

"I've got an idea that might help," Jim volunteered. "Perhaps I could ring a new contact in Ottawa. He works in the security service and apparently wants to get in touch with me anyway."

"Really? Great idea! It's a long shot, but if it is an international plot, they might well have gotten wind of something. Call now, the sooner the better, let's see what you can find out. We need to act fast, but I need a lot more information and some proof before I can contact CNN and break the story."

With that nudge, the Canadian picked up his cell phone and left the bar, leaving Robert to his own thoughts. Jim rang Ottawa knowing full well it was a longshot, but he was perplexed about why CISS had asked to speak with him and wanted to call them anyway. As he waited for the international call to go through, he reflected that there had been many changes in Ottawa since 9/11. The service had abandoned its primary tasks of supporting Canadian national interests in favour of helping the US regain its economic leadership in the world and defend its security in a global context. Its focus now was on Islamic terrorism and mafia money laundering. Was that why they wanted to speak to him?

Jim did not know who the man he was calling was or even what exactly he was hoping to get from him. But a line from Shakespeare suddenly came to him – *nothing will come of nothing*. Jim had learnt a long time ago that in this world there are no hard and fast rules. There are many voices of counsel but few of vision. He considered Robert to be one of the wise ones, but could he be totally trusted? Jim thought so. He also knew what had to be done, even though he couldn't do it himself. He felt obliged to do everything in his power to help.

The call to Ottawa went straight through.

"Wilcox here."

"Hello, this is Jim Johnson," he said in a staccato, diplomatic voice. "I understand you want to speak with me."

"Yes, we do." A mildly surprised voice answered. "I'll get right to the point. The Director wants to know if you are willing to leave the department of Global Affairs and join

CSIS as his Deputy Director. The Prime Minister has already given his approval."

"That's ridiculous! I have no experience in espionage."

"We know your background. We need you. I am able to offer you anything reasonable to get you to move over here. Let's start with your first request and then we can work out the details over the next few days."

"Well, I do have one immediate request. Do you people know anything about the Russians and Japanese collaborating with the French secret service to get control of large sectors of the French economy?"

There was a long pause. Then "Well it just happens that we do – but what is it to do with you? The Russians, the French security services and some corrupt businessmen on our radar have been meeting intensely for months. It has to do with money laundering – ski resorts and some kind of crooked land deal in France. But this is way over your pay grade." After a brief hesitation, he laughed and followed with, "Well, at least until you join us in CISS."

Jim explained that he had gotten wind of some shady dealings in Courchevel and that a friend who knew about it had been murdered. Larry Wilcox assured Jim that a CSIS official would ring him soon with more details. Jim in turned responded he would deeply consider the offer to join CSIS and the promise of a career enhancement. He wondered what his wife would think of him joining the tough guys in the spying world. No, he didn't wonder. He knew. She would not like it at all.

Jim felt unmoored at the prospect of a new job offer in the security service while a genuine crisis was developing right in front of him. He hoped Robert could handle it. He knew he couldn't help much because of his boys. He rang off and went back in the bar to tell Robert what he had learnt.

The new details from CSIS gave Robert all the evidence he needed. The plot was real. He accepted that Peter had been murdered because of what he had overheard at the Cat's bar. If he played it well, he should be able to expose the crooked dealings, foil the plot, and unveil the murderers. Adrenalin rushed through his veins. He felt alive again for the first time in years. With luck, he could shed his low moods, the 'black dogs' that had plagued him for three years now and get back into the real world. We are all required to go on, he told himself – not to be passive – but to act!

In his Oxford days, he had come to believe that many people were made of *crooked timber* and allowed bad things to happen. Since then, his journalism experience had confirmed that fact and taught him to distrust almost everyone. He had confidence in Jim. But could he trust himself?

Leadership requires optimism, competence and the ability to project drive and self-confidence. Robert knew that he had possessed some of these qualities at one time. He had shown them before. But did he still have them? Could he do this now? He had the bizarre thought that during the Cold War, the CIA's code name for MI6 was "uptight". Was he just an uptight weakling? In his self-doubt, he recalled a line from *Twelve Night – some are born to greatness, some acquire greatness, and some have greatness thrust upon them.* He grinned. *A bit pretentious*, he thought, *but this might be my only chance to make a comeback.*

Before Robert and Jim left Les Airelles, they had worked their way through several scenarios about how to proceed. In the end, they settled on a detailed plan that they thought was a good one. They hoped to confirm more details with Ottawa but, every time Jim tried to reconnect with his iPhone, the system was down. Robert speculated that this could be evidence that the French were tapping phones or blocking calls. Were the mafia on to him?

Just in case they were, he would go back to Méribel, but only briefly. He would not sleep there. After his usual dinner routine, he would come back by car and stay at the Courcheneige with Jim and his boys. This should give him enough time to gather any new information and enable him to escape the immediate notice of the mafia and security forces. Robert knew he should not go with Jim now in case he was already being followed. At dawn, he would leave and expose to the world what was going on here.

If, as he expected, telephone lines and the Internet were being intercepted, monitored or jammed, he needed another way to communicate. If he could get to the top of the Saulire, his satellite signal from there could not be blocked and he would be able to broadcast the story to the world via CNN, just like he used to do from Iraq and Syria. However, planning something is never dangerous but action is. Robert would need to evade any mafia who might follow him and then ski his way to success. It is in execution that the risks arise.

Robert had a pang of apprehension as he recalled that the thugs in his ski class were better skiers than he was. His mind raced. The element of surprise was vital. If, as he, suspected, he was being monitored by the French in cooperation with the Russians, he was in danger of ending up dead like Peter. These young goons would keep him in their sights and risk everything to kill him. *No matter how thin the pancake*, he thought with a sigh, *it always has two sides*. How could he escape their clutches long enough to tell the world what was going on in the Haute-Savoie and why they had killed his friend?

Chapter 10
The Great Chase

First light at Courchevel is one of the most beautiful sights on earth. On a clear morning, within a few seconds, the mountain peaks change their night's dark cloak to deep purple. Then gradually, only fleetingly, they take on a luminous pink as the rising sun reflects on the snow. As the sun rises higher, first the rocky slopes above the tree line, then the entire east slope of the mountain transforms itself. New snow becomes a brilliant virginal white, pure and untouched, beckoning the skier to partake of her delights even though only half awake and certainly not ready for much exertion.

Robert Arnett was awake for this first glimmer of light and rolled to the edge of his bed in the Courcheneige hotel room. Jim was still asleep, as were his two children in the loft. Robert knew that if he were going to succeed, he had to move quickly. If the henchmen had traced him here in spite of his precautions, they might harm Jim and his kids. He feared that they might have listened to tapes of his telephone conversations and surmised from them where he would be staying. He tried his cell phone. As he suspected, it was still dead, which meant the whole communication system of the area was down either because of the weather or, more likely, because of the intervention of the French security service.

He slid out of bed, silently pulled on his ski clothing and boots, and then slipped on the backpack that he had packed carefully earlier in Méribel. It contained his personal papers, maps, military flashlight, satellite telephone, and a miniature satellite dish. He had agreed with Jim last night that he would leave on his mission as early as possible this morning, just in case his would-be killers had found out where he was.

There was no other choice. Either he evaded the Russian goons now or he would be killed. That was the brutal reality. He felt a flush of adrenalin. Since he had been let go by CNN and especially after his wife died, Robert had hesitated to act on practically anything. He often reflected on the peaks and canyons of his life, on the capricious nature of fate and folly. But he had to admit, he was afraid. There was uncertainty and doubt. He knew he would have some time *hors-piste* and about ten minutes on a double-black diamond run – it was a brutal reality. Now that his adrenaline was flowing, however, he was focused and eager to take up the challenge.

As things stood, he knew that he alone was in a position to reveal the monstrous crime that was taking place and stop it in its tracks. He was still not sure how he would handle the extreme stress after all he had been through, but he recalled Edward R Murrow's admonition, *a nation of sheep soon has a government of wolves. I'm no wether* (castrated male sheep), he thought grimly, *even if I'm all too familiar with defeat and fear. I don't want to end on a grotesquely inadequate life. I don't believe in God but I sure miss him.*

Robert opened and shut the door softly and descended to the boot room to pick up his skis. He bristled with alarm, then anger, to find the ski equipment door locked – an unusual event, evidently a new routine to deter ski thieves. Robert glanced at his watch. He knew he could not wait until the attendant showed up. In desperation, he grabbed a pair of loose and mismatched skis that had been dropped off in the corridor. He had never tried to ski with one board longer than the other and wondered nervously what the effect would be.

He quickly and expertly adjusted the safety bindings on the uneven skis to fit his boots, marched out into the snow, and clicked into the bindings. He smiled. A Head and a Hart, one orange, one red. With one ski tip a few inches shorter than the other, he experimented with a kind of snow plough one way and a parallel turn the other. The snow was fairly deep and still ungroomed. Almost a half foot of it had fallen overnight and skiing in this lop-sided fashion was difficult and ridiculous at the same time. He smiled to himself. It was hilarious but doable. He was confident he could channel his anger and frustration into action.

Robert glanced up at the first light glowing on the peaks. He didn't even have the luxury of shadows yet. Thank God there was no one else on the slopes. But lights were starting to appear in some large chalets along the side of the run, including the one he believed to be the mafia's private *dacha* where the henchmen were probably staying. Indeed, within seconds one of the henchmen caught sight of the lopsided skier going down the Bellecôte run. He recognised Robert immediately and shouted, "There goes the bastard!"

He and his pal scrambled to dress as quickly as they could, having drunk too much vodka the evening before. One had been up most of the night with a severe case of diarrhoea while the other was highly constipated. They persevered, swearing as they pulled on their snow togs, grabbing their skis, and backpacks that were already crammed with phones and guns. Even in their delicate states, they were confident they could easily catch Robert. They were much stronger skiers than he was; they had outstripped him easily in the ski school.

By the time the two men arrived at the Croisette, the first lifts had departed and Robert had already gone. The goons guessed he would have taken the lift up the west side towards the Saulire because it always opened first to take supplies up to the restaurant. They took off their skis, raced up the stairs, flashed their *Trois Vallées* passes at the attendant and, against his protestations about the lifts not yet being open, grabbed the first one available.

While they had missed their opportunity to catch Robert on the Bellecôte, they knew it would only be a matter of time before they were within shooting distance. The French security service could contact them by walkie-talkie once they knew where he was headed. The men knew they would have to deal with the wrath of their crazy and vicious mafia boss if they missed him, but they had handled a lot harder jobs for Yuri than this one.

Meanwhile, Robert, who was nearing the top of the first Bubble lift, was studying the tattered, old ski map that had been stored in his backpack. He had been over the route in his mind all night and knew exactly where he needed to go but was not certain of the best way to get there, especially now given the snow conditions and his ridiculous skis. By the time the lift arrived at the second station, he was ready. When the doors opened, he sprinted to the large, new *téléphérique*. It was silent and no one was in sight. Robert looked around impatiently for an attendant. After what seemed like an eternity, a young Australian ski 'sweeper' showed up and began putting the huge machinery *en marche*.

The first and most important thing a skier does at a new resort is pick up and study a map of the area. The newest maps of Courchevel 1850 are colourful, and describe accurately the complete Three Valley terrain, with its 250 lifts and over a thousand runs. An up-to-date map of the ski trails and lifts is vital to ski safely in this area with its highly complicated system of villages, diverse lifts, restaurants, and hotels. Robert's trail map, however, was an old, well-used one that he had purchased many years ago. It had very small letters and a single colour. All the new maps describe the up-to-date routes he could take, but only the old map showed what he needed, the layout of the *former* ski station with its now old fashioned, by-passed lifts and runs.

Standing alone in the cavernous train-like ski lift, Robert used his military flashlight to check and re-check his route on the map, difficult as it was in the dim light with his hands shaking. His nervousness was tangible. As a seasoned journalist, he knew that if he could expose the international criminals and the French politicians who were linked to a corrupt secret group, he could foil their plot. They wouldn't dare act after they were publicly exposed. As a bonus, he might also be recognised by the media and perhaps even get his old job back as an international reporter with CNN. However, that daydream was quickly dashed by a more realistic assessment: the search for quick glory often leads to the grave.

Trouble was not far behind him. The gangsters reached the *téléphérique* station only shortly after Robert's car had left. Quickly assessing the situation, they ran to the equipment room, pushed aside the attendant and attempted, without success, to pull the emergency switch to stop Robert's cable car from reaching the second stop. The newly minted lift and the emergency system overrode their signal. In a futile effort, one took out his gun and fired at the ski car, but it was too far out of range.

Robert heard the shot. He could see how close the Russians were. Casting a frightened glance back at his pursuers, he left the lift swiftly the second it arrived at the top of the Saulire, clamped on his mismatched skis and headed for the notorious black corridor – the *couloir noir*. Meanwhile, the mobsters, infuriated at their helplessness, climbed into the next car to the top of the mountain.

Robert was confident of his plan. He had learnt about an abandoned ski lift that reached the top of a peak to the east of the Saulire in a French article he had read about two years ago. In a delightful scam, two teenagers had stolen some skis and then used the old lift to get to the top and the other side of the mountain for a clean getaway. Authorities had been perplexed. How could the thieves have escaped when the police had monitored all the lifts to the top the Saulire and on to Méribel? There were no other lifts from which they could have skied down to the other side of the mountain.

Eventually, they discovered that the enterprising thieves had used an old lift close to the *couloir noir* that had been abandoned years earlier when the modern cable cars were installed. It was no longer in general service, used only occasionally by emergency workers, and therefore did not show up on any recent maps.

Robert started down the steep *couloir* into what looked like an unholy abyss. He was so pumped he did not even notice the sub-zero temperature or contemplate how harrowing skiing would be on his bizarre skis. The powder was deep, and he was grateful that the ski instructor had pushed them so hard on Monday. He knew he should ski slowly because the light was still very poor, but he did not have that luxury. In the dark corridor, he could only distinguish between grey and black; there was simply no topographical relief as there would be later in the morning. Visibility was terrible and the killers were right behind him. *Is this how I die?* he wondered as he knew even the tiniest loss of control could be a disaster.

Robert took a deep breath and headed straight down, quickly reaching speeds just somewhat less than a downhill racer, in the range of 20–30 miles an hour for a couple minutes. He almost panicked when he realised that he was approaching his first marker where he needed to make an abrupt left turn. As he came around the curve, he could barely distinguish the precipitous change in the terrain. His heart leapt at the evidence that an avalanche had ripped through the area upending trees and boulders. "Shit!" he shouted as he planted his poles, jumped, and changed direction. He had always told himself that the cardinal rule in skiing was to follow your gut. He would. But it was dangerous. Any detour would take too much time.

For a few seconds, he felt comfortable again but he was also keenly aware that he was fast approaching a cliff where he would have to make a very quick, sharp turn. He sucked in his breath and tore across the path of the earlier avalanche. His new approach necessitated a 105 degree turn to the left

143

onto a cliffside path – an impossible task while moving on skis. As Robert approached the cliff's edge, he stopped abruptly near a huge boulder, jumped, and then quickly did a kind of shuttle manoeuvre until he had completed the required turn. His uneven tips barely showed above the snow. He then skied cautiously forward and soon began the last run of giant moguls on another double black diamond run. The faint light still afforded little relief on the landscape. It was difficult to tell up from down but he could feel the difference under his boots.

Back at the top of the Saulire, the mobsters had spotted Robert heading down the *couloir*. They fired twice at him but knew it was hopeless. They were still too far away for their revolvers or even their MP5s to hit him, and they had not brought their sniper rifles. In the lead, Dimitri yelled back, "Where is he going?" Yakof stopped and frantically consulted his new map. There was no time for the walkie talkie. He concluded that Robert would be forced to ski to the bottom of the *couloir* where there were various choices to work his way down to the Croisette or other lower areas.

It was a fatal mistake. They were unaware that Robert had already turned off the *couloir noir* and was headed *hors-piste* through the trees towards an unmarked lift. Although they were excellent skiers, they were less familiar than Robert with the Courchevel terrain, including the *couloirs* which took extreme skill and stamina at the best of times. The difficult run took their entire attention and they soon lost Robert's tracks.

By the time they arrived at the bottom of the run, they were exhausted and knew they had been tricked. Looking back up the mountain, they could see not only that no one was on the run but there were only two people's ski tracks in the snow. Where was he? Their high-powered guns were useless if they could not see him. Where was he headed? They called their French security contacts on their walkie-talkie. They knew their careers with the mafia would be over if they didn't stop Robert.

After his detour and abrupt move to the left onto the sharp path, Robert descended through some trees and then only halfway down the next run and then made another sharp turn to the left along a craggy pencil-thin ledge from which he could see an old, unused lift some 100 metres below. He skied straight to the old hut, and on arrival immediately broke a window, opened the door by an inside latch and entered the dilapidated building. Using his small military flashlight to find the start mechanism, he unleashed the ancient engine. To his joy, within seconds, he heard an awful, growling motor noise that signalled the lift was in motion. He quickly exited and clambered onto a small metal chair that took him to the top of the mountain.

On arrival, he ripped opened his backpack, knelt, and set up his equipment. He had not used his kit for image broadcasting since his time in Iraq and Syria, but it was still second nature to him. He first tried the cell phone but it was still unresponsive. Obviously, the French security officers in the village continued to jam the system. It was useless, so he opened the direct satellite transmission to CNN. Once connected, he felt the same surge of energy as he had experienced earlier in war zones. He was anxious, overly excited, and thinking far too fast, but he knew exactly what he had to do.

On contact with the CNN producer, he explained he was Robert Arnett, former member of their foreign affairs team, and that he had an exclusive international "breaking news" story. With care, he summarised what he knew of the plot slowly and accurately. The senior producer who vetted the story quickly recognised its value and rushed it to air. Within moments, Robert's breaking news and picture were beamed around the world.

A lone CNN hero had uncovered an international conspiracy and a sinister plot to buy up France's cultural heritage, the prestigious French ski area south of Geneva. It was all done to enrich a Japanese corporation, a French businessman and local politicians, as well as Russian oligarchs supported by the mafia and their Moscow leaders. The French Minister of the Interior and President Marchand were allegedly implicated. International terrorists, probably ISIS, were involved but their names and affiliations could not be confirmed at this time.

Once this shocking information hit the airwaves, everyone got into the act. Within minutes, social media commentators outside the Courchevel area generated millions of tweets and Facebook comments, many of which were inaccurate but politically explosive. *ISIS has captured parts of France*, the most ludicrous shrieked. Within hours, local French journalists were rushing to Courchevel, international newsmen and women also were *en route*, including slim brunette female journalists from CNN and a blond leggy one from Fox news.

Talk programs soon showed pictures of the French Alps with commentary from American newsmen and statesmen who had skied there long ago in their youth. They expressed incredulity that such a take-over was possible, and offered exiguous commentary and advice. Opposition politicians in the French National Assembly called an emergency meeting to start the unlikely proceedings to impeach President Marchand.

The accidents and murders that had come close to undermining French ownership of the ski villages had ceased. The international plot dissolved. Their cover-up was impeccable. In the end, none of the principal conspirators was charged, but two jihadi females were arrested on suspicion of murder. ISIS was blamed. Rumour had it that the organisation had unleashed a terror plot in Courchevel but had been intercepted by security forces. The French politicians and businessmen were cleared of any wrongdoing in the affair. The Japanese connection was not pursued and the Russians had long gone and left no trail of wrongdoing.

After an interlude of sheer terror, the bizarre plot was over and Robert Arnett was a genuine American hero. He had channelled his anger and frustration into action and found success at the intersection of random chance, talent, and hard work. He had made luck happen.

Chapter 11
Snow and Sun

Christmas arrived in the Alps. The day dawned with a partial sun and quarter moon racing to decorate the sky. The sun transformed the mountain, replacing its cloak of darkness with creepy shadows, then brilliant mysterious light. At the summit, a triple rainbow painted a happy omen with their trajectories into the valley of the Creux.

A new ski day began and with it the unending search for excitement, thrills, and happiness resumed. In just a few months, like clockwork, the snow would begin to melt and the first signs of spring would arrive. Heavy wet snow and silvery icicles dripping from the trees and eaves would be followed by bare patches that would reveal the secrets of winter, rocks, mud, and the remains of human events that had transpired over the winter. The enigmatic cycle would begin again.

On Christmas day, all was well on the surface. It was time to rejoice. Church bells pealed and thanks were offered in the local church. It was time to forget and move on. People ate, drank, danced, made love, rejoiced and skied. They longed to return to the life they knew and loved. Nothing from the past few days seemed real.

The weather gods were no longer disturbed and all the nightmarish threats had vanished into thin air. Violent crimes had been committed, not in the name of politics or ideology, but for the sole purpose of greed and making money. There was no single villain or unblemished police. Guilt was not as clear or self-evident as in cases of common domestic crime or even traditional international conflict, terrorism, or war. The Cold War was far in the past and the new international economy, with its accompanying global criminality, enabled money, both legal and illegal, to swish around easily between countries and continents, tempting voracious entrepreneurs everywhere to join in the competition for money and wealth.

A deep blanket of snow still covered everything except the few human tragedies that had been openly revealed – the bloody murder of Peter Worthington, the slaughter of a cleaning lady in her yellow car, the dozens of skiers hurt or killed in staged accidents. These had been the handiwork of the Russian mafia, greedy French businessmen and political leaders who by now were nowhere to be found. Their tracks were well covered. They suffered no consequences. The entropy of the pre-Christmas ski week was over.

The police concentrated on each crime separately, not recognising the novel and implicit interconnections among jihadis, mafia, corrupt politicians, and unethical businessmen. As time goes by, we all learn that we live in stable prisons of the mind. All significant change is difficult to understand. Contrary to the impression given in traditional simple thrillers or mystery novels or Hollywood movies that focus narrowly on menacing individuals in specific countries, current international conspiracies and crimes involve complex transnational groups. Criminals and terrorists are no longer

149

primarily confined to any one country or area or party ideology. Their victims are unwary protagonists everywhere in the world. And, with the advancement of modern communications and contemporary culture the world is being desensitised to people taking and posting ego satisfying 'selfies' to boast and document their deeds, even when they entail such horrors as maiming and killing people.

In Othello, the hero concludes, *We must obey the time*, before killing Desdamona. He then commands, "Put out the lights," as he snuffs out the candle. Some things never change. In Shakespeare's perceptive plays, both great and lowly people are brought down by their foibles, and especially by their willingness to engage in extreme behaviour for personal gain. Jolly satire dominates.

The relentless transformation of culture and character in the global world creates a new public sense of confusion and terror. Political and philosophical ideals collapse under the pressure of action and circumstance. Modern international affairs is depicted by hot but shallow television commentators in contemporary social media as dramatic theatre with stereotypical characters and marionette actions by diplomats, politicians, and others.

A series of great snowstorms opened this ski season in France, but by Christmas, despite tragedies and ugly revelations, the sun returned and people began to ski again. There was no expiation. Evidence of wrongdoing disappeared. All traces of the murders and accidents were gone. Happiness resumed on the surface of the snow.

By Christmas week, revellers did not know or care very much about how French politicians had been willing to sell out their country for personal profit. The Russian mafia had fled, if only temporarily, leaving little trail of their wrongdoing. The unseen international businessmen had covered their tracks and moved on to other schemes in far off countries. De Rothschild continued to prowl for new sexual exploits. The Japanese connection was not pursued by the police. The French politicians knew what they could get away with and why. All were cleared of criminal wrongdoing. A culture of commercial corruption, new conspiracies, and selfishness continued. Only the two female jihadis, whose husbands had been killed in an America raid in Syria, were held in custody, arrested on suspicion of terrorist activities.

People always defend happiness as a goal – ideals are central to its pursuit. As time goes by, and tragedies unfold, the transcendent nature of human purpose lives on without interruption. Humans strive to understand and overcome the human predicament of life and death. They make choices and try to do things their own way.

But while the belief in happiness includes the importance of the individual and free choice, celebration and commitment to the life of the intellect, vocation, and achievement are less celebrated. Many of life's moral and ethical choices, even, or perhaps especially, at Christmas at a ski resort, are buried and ignored beneath much clutter. In the bold ambiguity of events at Courchevel 1850 that year, even determining who the enemy was proved difficult.

As usual in Courchevel 1850, Christmas day was celebrated by a great torch-lit parade. In the late afternoon, the whole community gathered around the Croisette. The rich from Courchevel 1850, the bourgeois from the regional hotspots and the humble lower classes from the lowest villages down the mountain joined as one. Cries of joy rung out and they rejoiced in a frenzy with the first rockets of fireworks. Mulled wine, beer, liquor, and hot chocolate flowed copiously. Twinkling lights adorned the buildings. Glitter and balloons decked the buildings and stairways. Red, white, and blue streamers were wrapped around pylons and streetlamps. French flags flew everywhere, especially in shop windows. The turbulence of the frenzied crowd with its happy faces and flushed cheeks and noisy merrymakers wiped out the miseries of the past few days.

As the day wore on, the Bubble lifts carried more than a hundred ski monitors up to the top of the Vizelle peak to ski down in long rows, following crazily dressed parade marshals. They all carried torches to light their way down the runs. The mountain soon would be magically alight as they decorated the *pistes* with their fire. Meanwhile, at the base, a fashion show began with skiers in costumes parading in fashionable clothes from the 1789 French revolution.

Watching the show with sheer delight were four particularly joyous non-French spectators. Jim Johnson, a Canadian, who had just been made Deputy Director of Canada's security services was with his two pre-teen boys taking in the glorious show with laughter. Joining them in the festivities was Robert Arnett, an American who was rapidly becoming famous around the world for breaking the CNN story about corruption and murder in Courchevel 1850.

A local band with clanging cymbals broadcast a boisterous French national anthem on loudspeakers throughout the village. Scantily clad, nubile skiers swayed to the loud, optimistic, and patriotic music of basses, drums, and wind instruments. As usual, war and terrorism are not defeated by literature but by popular jokes, songs and verse.

Then, as rare as the bloom of a single red rose in the winter or the sighting of the first flight of a fledgling golden eagle, the nearly impossible happened.

Just as the torchlight parade and brilliant fireworks ended and the band exploded once more into the final bars of the French Marseillaise, a totally nude skier clad only in bright red ski boots descended alongside the Olympic ski jump. He skied gracefully, turned to face the hundreds of spectators lining the run, and slalomed through the heart of the Croisette, wagging his way to the magisterial sound of *Marchons, Marchons.*

The audience roared with astonishment and laughter, and much to everyone's surprise broke in unison into their own rendition of the French national anthem. The unidentified, nude skier sped over the small moguls, completed the remainder of the short run through the village, slid through the icy underpass, and disappeared over the slopes to Courchevel 1550, Le Praz, or perhaps St Bon.

Christmas ski week was over. The sinister undercurrent of Courchevel had been replaced by a jolly satire in the bright light of a massive cultural and criminal upheaval.